£2·50
/23

THE QUIET TRUTH

SHARON THOMPSON

BLOODHOUND
— BOOKS —

Print ISBN 978-1-913942-14-4

ALSO BY SHARON THOMPSON

The Abandoned

The Healer

To the magic.
For Victoria.

1

CHARLIE QUINN

I shouldn't be taking this child up a quiet country lane but I never mean any harm. The wafts of an Irish summer breeze wisp her fine brown hair back from her pudgy cheeks. I've waited a long time to tell the truth. With Faye's chubby fingers curled around mine, it is time to begin.

'We thought you must have died. Nothing for sixty years, Charlie?'

I'm supposed to answer questions like these. Instead, I leave, shrug, or sigh. It's easier to be silent than to spill the secrets of a lifetime. There's a lot of goodwill for me in these cooped-up rooms. Generations find my silence charming and endearing. I'm fortunate to be accepted back with little explanation or excuses.

The darkest of souls are the quietest, yet these strangers take my silence as gentlemanly – a quirk from being away for years from the Irish chatter and craic. All I want is to be roaming free on the Canadian prairies again. Ireland's air and the grass verges have not changed – the electricity poles are new.

Did I walk calmly away when I left all those years ago? Or

did I run towards the shore or the mountains? I know that my feet moved a damn sight easier than they do now.

The toddler babbles and my seventy-eight-year-old heart leaps listening to the nonsense. It's a glorious sound that only the innocence of life can make. If this generation knew of the secrets in my past would they let me wander away with their most precious future gripping my wizened finger?

Squinting into the sun I remember with a pain in my chest how I never heard our own child make much noise. I'm sure Ella tried to convince them of her innocence. No one listened. It seems that she protected me from the truth. There's no knowledge of what I did or didn't do. I'm here to change all of that.

It is hard being back. Like Oisin in the Irish legend, I've returned from the Land of Youth to find almost everyone important to me has gone. Thankfully, the woman I've come home for is most definitely alive.

Even after all this time, my darling Ella's name is dragged up. Someone mentioned 'that Ella O'Brien' outside the shops this very morning. The venom lingered in the wind and still I said nothing.

As usual, Charlie Quinn keeps quiet.

I can see my Ella smiling. Her full lips pucker to mine.

Suddenly, I run away from those blue eyes and leave her to fend them all off. Sixty years ago, I scuttled away like a rat.

A car passes us. The occupant waves and strains to see the stranger on the grass verge with a small child. In many ways, this part of Ireland hasn't changed. There's little that goes unnoticed on country lanes. What is being said now about me since I've returned? The welcomes have been sincere and hemmed with a tinge of concern. After all of these years, Charlie Quinn came back to them and he doesn't talk as much as he should.

The child's mother is called Rhonda and her kitchen stifled me with the smell of roast beef. I took off into the sunshine.

'Had my mammy cooked such nice things I may have stayed but we were dirt poor, pious Plymouth brethren from Tyrone,' I tell Faye as we amble on. 'You're lucky not to be one of those. I never understood their minds and ways. You have a lovely home here in Sligo.'

'Yes,' the child says and toddles a bit further without my assistance. She's a good listener; even if she's not much of a talker. We're alike.

It's not lost on me that an old man prefers the company of a two-year-old child. The women in my life might agree that I am childish. Bones creak and groan at me. In my marrow I'm still the eighteen-year-old boy who left the Irish lanes and fields in 1930 for something new.

The Sligo air is clear, fresh and cool. I've missed that air. The green fields don't spread out as much. In my memory the squares were bigger. Like the population the grass is cordoned off, owned and surrounded in stone.

'Claustrophobia,' the doctor told me it was called and I was delighted to hear it was a condition that others had. From when Father barricaded me in the barrel out the back of the byre, I knew that small spaces and me were not friends.

I suppose it wasn't my father's fault. I had been bad again and needed locked away. He was a man with morals and a sense of fatherhood, which I never inherited. He tried to make me good. I failed him over and over.

'I'm a coward, child.'

'Yes,' she mutters again and looks up at me.

Had our child dark or blue eyes? I don't know. Ella must have hated me. I promised her everything. Did anyone else suspect? They must have.

Oddly, there's not a whisper of it – not a flinch of recognition when Ella is mentioned now.

'Weren't you here though, Charlie, when that woman was in

3

the papers the first time? You know, about *that Ella O'Brien*? Weren't you living here back then when it happened? It's all back in the news recently. My own mother remembers your brother coming here to Sligo to get away from it all in the North and he brought all these newspaper clippings. He was telling us about how you lived so close to the O'Briens. He couldn't get over how she showed no remorse. You left Tyrone around then too, eh? Weren't you lucky. Fierce goings-on,' Rhonda, my host says.

Still it lingers in the minds of communities. I search their eyes for traces of connections between me and the married, older beauty. There are none. They are simply remarking about the latest media interest. That is all that stirs their gossip. I am free in the open, but locked away inside; eaten-up with the lies and the failings.

Like this child with me now I'm still being led by my fate, taken by the hand and marched into danger.

What might they all do when they know the truth? What will happen to the endearing old Charlie Quinn when it all becomes clear? Putting things right has dragged me across the Atlantic Ocean. I may be bitterly disappointed and I will shock those who've taken me in.

I sit on the stile that should take us into the field and the child stops to suck on a blade of grass. It might tear her tiny lips and I let her do it anyway. The daisies dance up at me from between her tiny shoes.

'We hadn't meant to harm anyone,' I tell the top of the child's head. 'It's not something we planned and it tore our lives asunder. I was a boy myself and I didn't know what I was doing.' There's liquid dripping from my chin and I swipe at it with my suit's sleeve. I urge a tie away from my throat. 'You've got to believe me. They've all got to. Despite everything I've done in this life I'm not a bad man.'

'Yes,' the child says suddenly and she makes a string of sounds that end in a word which sounds very like, *bad!*

My old fingers curl under her chin and I stoop lower to make her look at me. She lets me do it, babbling on, ignoring my torment, paying no heed to the man who could stop her breathing. If she's a sign of what the universe thinks of old Charlie Quinn, then I'm finished.

'Bad, bad, bad.' She stomps those little shoes and spits out the grass. The screams of Ella were loud enough to break the haze I was in and even now they pierce my ears. It takes a child to see the real Charlie Quinn.

'I am sorry. Ella, I'm very sorry it has taken me this long to come home.'

It is the child who is crying. Fear clouds her scrunched-up face and drowns her cheeks. She's twisted in my arms, writhing homewards and breathing heavily, kicking her heels back and out against my old arms and grasp.

I'm crying, as my spectacles steam and become laden in drops. I can hear someone calling up the road. 'Charlie, is everything all right? Have you got Faye with you?'

I drop the child onto the grass verge, and turn towards the sea. Even if I could, I cannot run and the sounds of cries and her father promising her that he's coming to get her makes me heave out vomit over the stile.

Her father picks her up and pats my back, muttering to us both, 'It will all be all right. Don't cry. Charlie, are you okay? What's brought this on?'

I want to tell him that nothing has ever been right with Charlie Quinn. Like the poor innocent toddler knows, Charlie Quinn is bad, bad, bad. I take off my glasses and blur the world as I heave my shirt tails out to clean away evidence of my guilt.

'What's up?' the child's father asks me. I think he's called Joe. 'Sure you must be wrecked. Everyone wants to know so much and it must be...' He coughs, uncomfortable at finding me upset. If only he knew, I deserve hell itself.

'Bad, bad, bad,' Faye screams.

'How right she is.' I sniff. 'I'm a bad man.'

'I doubt that, Charlie. Rhonda will love to hear all about your life. Take it all in your own time. She doesn't have to work on it right this minute.' The man has to shout over Faye's sobs. 'We've got the dinner ready. Let's get something warm into you.'

I sense it's been leaked out that I'm dying of cancer. At my age it's hardly a surprise and considering I'm a monster it makes total sense that I'm being eaten from the inside out. This is a just punishment for all that I've done. In their eyes I'm vulnerable and in need of looking after. That adds to the guilt and the bulbous cancer growths. They swell with each kind gesture. The irony is not lost on me – I'm being killed with kindness.

We make it back to the homestead without a word. The crying of the toddler eases into the man's shoulder. His pretty wife accepts my tired hand into hers on the doorstep with a sympathetic nod.

If only she knew what these hands have done. I shuffle to their downstairs bathroom and let the soap suds wash away the last few hours. The remaining members of my stranger-family wait seated around the ordered tableware and bowls of steaming food. All of them are looking expectantly at me as I enter the room.

The child's mother is some sort of relation. I cannot remember who she came out of or to whom she belongs. It doesn't matter anyhow.

I slump into the chair and she raises her voice towards me. 'You lived in a time, Charlie, where children had more freedom. We were worried when you took Faye with you. Perhaps let us know if you go out again?' I listen and want to offer an explanation but there isn't one. She's trying to be kind and there's a forced politeness to her voice as she says, 'I cannot wait to hear all about your life. I'm thrilled that you're going to stay here for a while and let me write about you.'

The toddler's got a runny nose and she rubs it against my bony knee, smudging snot into the material. She smiles up, either forgetting or forgiving me for making her afraid.

'My child's eyes were dark,' I tell the table of strangers who are somehow blood to me. 'That's what I remember most now.'

There's a silence and a 'yes' from the tiny presence at my knee.

'You don't know who I am,' I tell them all. 'There's a lot about me that you won't want to know. And still... it's time to tell the truth.'

2

CHARLIE QUINN

The dinner goes on while I cry into the serviette and make it into a sodden mess. The wine glass is refilled and my plate is whisked away before I embarrass the hostess by not eating a bite.

There is an odd pat on my arm and a squeeze of my shoulder and they talk on about the weather, Ireland's unusual soccer success in the World Cup, Haughey as Taoiseach and the reunification of Germany. I have very little to contribute and the child clings to my knee. She is not removed from there.

Every pause in my sobbing takes me to think on all that remains unsaid and to the pain of what is to come. Their looks of pure curiosity bring me back to the sadness in my soul. Someone suggests that I move from the table but unless I can be transported out of the country there seems no reason to move at all. My discomfort is not something I can control and each heave of emotion should be the last. All should remain silent and fine – but no, I heap out cry after cry and wet napkin after napkin, while they all pretend life is grand.

'I'm an old fool,' I tell the child. 'Faye, I'm sorry.'

The dessert is ice cream and I manage some. Faye climbs

into my lap and I feed her off my spoon and the 'awws' fill the room.

'You'll be fine, Charlie,' their voices say. 'You're home now.'

'Home,' I whisper to Faye.

'She wants to make you better,' Rhonda, the child's mother, says. In my youth I would have liked Rhonda's femininity and flirted with her. I would have wanted her for my own. Marriage never meant much to me, and now I see her only as a means to an end. A way of being free of the past. She'll help place my life in black and white. I'll confess. Perhaps, with her help I will atone. I'm grateful to this woman and I couldn't eat the lovely meal she made. That makes me sad too.

'Faye likes you, Charlie,' Rhonda adds.

'I've always been good with the ladies.' Not a hint of a wink comes from me as it is the first real truth since I crossed her threshold.

My mother adored me. I was most certainly her favourite. Even when my youngest sister came to grace us twin boys with her annoying presence, Mother said that I still had stolen her heart. She found it hard to love the rest and she whispered this to me and a few close allies who visited to buy her eggs. Father discouraged friendships outside of the brethren. We were an oddity to ourselves as well as others. Mother married him because she was told to. In my father's eyes she showed vanity and longed for music and colour in her life. Father swayed between lust of her youthful beauty and his need to keep her *moral*.

Now, I watch Faye carry her small patchwork blanket and recall the tattered one they covered my mother in. Whether she walked into the quarry's lake, or jumped, fell or was pushed – they were never certain. Of course, I knew the truth.

Cedric and I whispered while crouched under the stairs that maybe Father had held her too long under the water in the barrel out at the back. He didn't usually do that to Mother, and he didn't seem surprised when she was brought back to us all wet and covered up. We knew him very well for we'd spent ten years avoiding him. As twins we also knew each other best and although Cedric was always good, I was like his evil other half. I was often called that and it became almost natural to adopt that role. I protected Cedric and young Anna as best as I could from the fervent zeal of a man lost in his own versions of right and wrong.

'When will we start?' I ask Rhonda as she clears the dishes into the sink. 'I suppose we start with my birth?'

The other unimportant Sligo relations have left, shaking my hand without me really being at the other end of it. Faye is sleeping somewhere. I was told these things when I awoke from a short snooze. There'd been drool on my chin and I had heard it mentioned that I was going to be 'a handful'.

It's time for me to be a gracious guest. Taking a deep breath I say, 'You're very good to take me in. We're not tightly related. Your grandfather, Arnold, was a cousin to my father. That's not exactly close, eh? And here you are giving me meals and a comfortable bed. I promise I won't outstay my welcome. Visitors are like fish. They go off.'

'The whole Quinn clan stretching from Tyrone and Sligo are glad that you're back and we're all curious about you too. So, I'll like listening to that nice voice of yours and enjoy knowing more.' That charm she works on others would have worked wonders on me years ago. I wish I still had my pecker. Being with Rhonda brings all that desperate-old-man-longing back.

'Mother died in her apron,' I say.

The startled look in Rhonda's eyes tells me she knows

nothing about my Tyrone childhood. She seems only aware of the romantic nonsense the family grapevine has probably curled out of somewhere and trickled across counties and family trees.

'Yes, my twin, Cedric, and I were about ten when my mother drowned... and she was still wearing her apron. For a particular woman this was not right. My mother would have taken it off to greet a house-caller and would have taken it off to go anywhere.'

'Gosh.' Rhonda sits on the sofa too. I never remember couches being this big in Ireland. She seems very far away and her perfume is nice. Her legs are a lovely kind of slender. 'Mammy's leg stuck out from under the blanket they covered her in.'

'I'll get my old tape recorder for this. Wait just a minute.'

I lean my grey, balding head against the sofa and take off my spectacles. My mind throbbed with guilt then and now. Mother probably stood up for me, or spoke up on my behalf, and he hurt her. Cedric and I both thought that in the dark stuffiness near Father's old boots under the stairs. We both said that it was no accident.

'It's in my blood, you see. The badness,' I tell Rhonda when she returns. 'They said Mother might have jumped into that quarry lake. That isn't correct. She wouldn't have worn her apron. He killed her and got away with it. I suppose from then I felt if my father could do that – then so could I. He cared so much about religion and right and wrong. He stopped our mother from breathing and nothing happened to him at all. If he could do that to a fine woman, then why couldn't I do worse?'

'Your mother, this is, and you think that your father got away with what, Charlie?' I can tell Rhonda's excited already. She's lustful for what I might blurt out next. I suppose it is salacious. Northern Ireland seventy years ago was a boring enough place. It still can be a grey dismal hole where nothing really seems to happen. A young mother drowned in her apron. Nothing happened. I must have nodded at Rhonda's question as she seems happy not to ask me anything else. She's smiling, like little Faye might. They do resemble each other. I don't look like anyone at all. I didn't even resemble my twin brother.

I can tell that Rhonda trusts me. Lord love her, because I don't trust myself. Is it fair to burden her with this? It isn't like the fiction she's used to. It isn't like she can unhear what is to come, and what will happen when she knows it all? What will become of those looks of interest, those sympathetic gestures, those caring touches on my arm and the cups of sweet tea?

'How about you just talk? I won't interrupt,' she suggests after a while of silence. 'Joe's cutting the lawn before it rains. I know you want this to be between us for now. Faye will hopefully sleep for a while. You've tired her out. Where might you start?'

'Have I not already started?' I snap and immediately regret it.

'Yes,' she mutters. 'You have indeed started, Charlie.' She sips at the herbal tea she drinks. I'm grateful my sense of smell is not as it should be, for I know those tea-potions can reek to high heaven. 'Tell me more, please. Maybe, more about what your father did.'

'I don't think I can go over all that again.'

'Then tell me about Cedric and yourself. A twin brother must've been nice to have? I remember Cedric, he's been dead a few years. Were you close as children?'

Cedric never mentioned me at all then. I don't need to ask her if he did or not. I know from listening since I came home that my name hasn't been uttered in many years. The bad things have not circulated. I should be grateful for this blessing, but it stings that Cedric and Anna just left me out of their lives. It seems too, that Mother's existence was wiped from the family consciousness as well. Whether she jumped, walked or was pushed into the water, she was stupid or weak and therefore is no longer spoken of.

Father started that mantra from the day and hour she was placed into the ground. We were forbidden to cry or call out for her in our sleep. Elizabeth, or Beth Quinn was to be no more. When I left, it seems the same happened to Charlie Quinn.

Both of us aren't even memories.

I must be talking as Rhonda is nodding sympathetically, urging me to keep going. I close my eyes and Cedric's playful, chatty voice greets me in the darkness under the stairs. The scent of old boots, the feel of the straw-brush under my fingers, the singing of Anna somewhere else in the house as Father is at work.

Still to this day, I'm not sure what Father did to earn his meagre wages. As a child he simply went out and did something. Even into adulthood it wasn't discussed and I cared very little about what took him away for a few hours every day, bar a Sunday.

I was glad of his absence. Cedric might've known what Father's job was. Cedric was intuitive and cared about others. Anna and Cedric were quite similar. They toiled with the chores Father shared out. They did mine too so I would be saved a wigging or a trashing. I never liked writing or reading, although I found both easy. Counting money made me happy. Anna trailed after us on adventures. Cedric was kind and I threw stones to make her return home.

Of course, there was a replacement mother in the years after the leg under the blanket was buried. This next poor woman was not the evil stepmother I hoped she'd be. The poor soul was quiet and docile and, of course, I was cruel when she tried to be good to us all.

I don't remember now exactly what I did to her. I know I refused to wash if she wanted me to and did nothing she suggested. Cedric thrived under her skirt tails, following the woman about. He did anything she needed. Father never talked over her and I wondered what she did to his spirit. He was a different man. It wasn't until I fell in love myself that I understood what happened to him. Her name escapes me now. Nothing comes to mind about the poor woman. Not even a sense of what she looked like. Isn't it awful that I don't remember things? Perhaps I don't want to as my own dear mother isn't remembered?

I've gone through life angry. It started from then. There's always been a knot in my gut. I hold on to my protruding paunch which is more from the cancer than good living, and think on the anger that swelled inside all of my life.

There have only been a few times where I didn't have a twist in my insides, and I've had only a few precious people take me out of that horrible feeling.

I point to my heart and decide it is time to say it out loud.

'I haven't been close to many people in my life. It was Ella O'Brien who took me out of being churned up in here.'

RHONDA IRWIN

F aye likes Charlie Quinn. Joe finds him fascinating. My radar for bad men is not working as it should. I know it isn't.

Women sense things and, of course, we must pretend that we don't. I've turned the volume on my intuition down. I need to get back to work; journalism, writing, making a pound – whatever you want to call it. And, I think that Charlie is my way to write again.

'Stop panicking,' Joe said before this Charlie Quinn arrived. 'We aren't starving. I'll take care of us.'

I wanted to believe my gorgeous Joe with his floppy brown hair, perfect face and slim arse. He's a good 'un in all the ways that matter.

'A great catch,' the relations thought and then there's the usual comment, 'like undertakers, we'll always need an accountant. He'll marry you someday now that the baby is here.'

The lack of commitment hurts and instead of saying that, I pretend being unwed suits my artistic temperament. Joe's dreams have been the same as my own. He was to be a writer. A novelist if truth be told. He both encouraged and resented the bit of success I've had. Being published was everything to us both. And my debut was my first baby. There wasn't much fuss and the money my novel brings in is paltry for the amount of tears I've shed. This drives the despair deeper.

'You've achieved. Stop with the self-loathing,' Joe says. And although he does introduce me as, 'My nest egg in the making. We're waiting on Hollywood to call for the film rights to Rhonda's work,' there is a tinge of sarcasm there too. I ignore it. Mostly, I let things slide. Good women do that.

We live in rural Sligo and women are meant to be a certain way. 'Smile, it might never happen,' a man said to me in the local shop yesterday. I slapped on a smile and walked the two tiny aisles talking myself out of stabbing him between the eyes with the screwdriver that lay beside the air-fresheners and the bleach.

'I'll try to be happy,' I said without a hint of bitterness. I'm getting good at hiding reality.

'Your hair has always been thick,' my mother says. 'It'll come back. This is all just the blues after a baby, Rhonda. The good Lord will see you through these sad times. He'll forgive you for having a child out of wedlock. Pray.'

Screaming into my mother's face happened in my head but I nodded and murmured, 'Yes.'

I sin a lot – Joe and I shagged far too often before Faye came along. It was what we did best. We were at it like rabbits until I peed on a stick. Since Faye there hasn't been much lovemaking.

And praying about things – HA! That's what got me into this mess.

I watched Charlie slurp his breakfast cereal with Faye this morning and realised that I'd asked for this odd man too. 'One more big story, God, please. One more interesting topic to get me back into print. Send me something good. I need to be writing and to be back in the saddle. I know I prayed for Faye and now she's here I wouldn't send her back no matter how hard it seems. I just need a bit more. It's hard to explain. I want my old life back. I want to be Rhonda Irwin again. Please, send me an escape. A reason to succeed. I'll not ask for anything again.'

I lie to myself and to the big man in the sky. I always ask for more. There's never a balance.

'You're the prettiest girl about here, big hair and round brown eyes. I'd kill for your figure. I was never that well-endowed. Joe never left you despite it all. Yes, it would be good to be married, but until then you'll have to learn to be content,' my mother sings at our family dinners. She makes it sound easy to do. Considering she's never been happy, I doubt it is. Since Dad left she has found her equilibrium; golfing, cycling club and baking buns for the church's bake sales. 'You've a healthy baby, a good handsome man, a happy home – what is the matter with you? If you want to get married and stay that way – then smile and be nice once in a while.'

I see Charlie watching Joe and I. He does it often. It's unnerving. Of course, Joe thinks he's just happy to be amongst his own people again. I see those old grey eyes brimming with something – is it gratitude? I'm not sure.

'The poor divil is overwhelmed. Give him a break, Ronnie. He's jet-lagged and sick. What on earth do you expect? Not everyone gushes with their innermost thoughts and feelings. Be patient for once in your life and let the old man be.'

Even Joe was flummoxed by the display at the family dinner table. 'Crying. Continuous sobbing. It should have broken us all into tears. I dunno, you're right, there was something selfish about it. It made me uneasy.'

Mum had been unchristian about it too. 'There's a time and a place for that kind of thing. I was cringing for him. And you'd made such an effort. And for once, Rhonda, you had cooked the meat to perfection and sure, it was all ruined. He's going to be a handful. Get him talking and back on that plane as soon as possible.'

'He took Faye,' I said to Joe as we undressed for bed. 'And suddenly all in a wave, I saw how much I loved her. You know? Like, how much she means to me. Like, if she wasn't here anymore what would I do?'

Joe opened and closed his mouth. I noticed that he was still handsome. That chest I love was bare and beautiful. I could tell that he thought I'd made an awful admission. Once it was out, I thought that too.

'I know it shouldn't take something scary for me to understand things. I know I'm a bad mother in your eyes and everyone else's.'

'Stop, Ronnie. This isn't about you. Not everything is about you.'

I went on folding my clothes. 'I mean it brought some things home. You don't think he'd harm her, do you?'

Joe wrenched off his socks. 'Having Charlie here was your idea,' he said in that annoying tone he has. 'He's a great man, you said. Jesus, Ronnie, you change your mind like the frigging wind. What do you want now?'

'My fault again,' I reply.

'If the cap fits!'

'You said it would be good for me to have him here.' I sound childish.

'Did I? You said it would be good for *you*. I said nothing. As per usual, I went with what you said you wanted.'

'Well, then. It's not my fault. You should have spoken up and told me what you thought.'

'And when might I have done that? You decided the minute you heard he was home that there was a story behind all of this. You were the one to grab it as some big exclusive nonsense. When was I supposed to have an opinion?'

'You know I can smell out a story. I'm good at that – give me that much at least.'

'You used to be good at a lot of things.' His voice slows.

'What do you mean?'

'Not that long ago you were a good lay.'

I stand there in my underwear and wonder do I even like Joe anymore.

'Sorry,' he mutters, not meaning the word.

'You always throw sex at me in an argument. It takes two to bonk, you know. This isn't all my problem.' I fling my jeans into a ball. Fuck him!

'Once you've written this story, or book or whatever you're planning... can we go back to the way things were? Please?' Joe throws his other smelly sock with emphasis onto the floor. 'When Charlie is gone promise me that we will be like we were again, yes?'

'I want that too.' A part of me wants to ask Joe if he still loves me. If he ever loved me at all.

We look at each other and he smiles first. 'We'll get through this,' he says.

'I...'

When tossing and turning in bed, I hear a snore from the guest bedroom. If I can hear Charlie snore, can he hear us fighting? It's doubtful.

I should also turn the volume on my intuition back up, then I might know the truth about Joe and I. Best not to do anything right now. I'll leave things be.

4

CHARLIE QUINN

I've made the conversation to suit my audience. I can tell that Rhonda will like an old romantic tale. She'll prefer the love story rather than the one I should be telling. She's scribbling and nodding when I do chance a glance at her. The sound of a distant lawnmower cuts through the Sunday afternoon.

Father wouldn't let us do anything on a Sunday. Nothing at all. Us children would find our fun away from him and the mammy he'd brought home.

We'd take off up the lanes and fields, find frogspawn in ponds or try to catch fish in the streams. For hours we travelled on foot and didn't think about it. We weren't told off or sent home. There was plenty of dirt and we didn't notice being rained upon. Cedric was the one to announce, 'Home soon.' And we'd obey. Anna and I didn't even think to ask how he knew the time.

It was a Sunday that I first saw her. My Ella O'Brien. She was by the side of the road picking wild tulips and placing them into her wicker basket. She had a bicycle but she wasn't riding it that day. She was all alone and we decided to spy on her.

It was the early summer of 1926 and Cedric and I were fourteen. Sunday was our time away from the confines of life and we enjoyed the play-acting we got up to. I was to start my trade the following year and our childhood was slipping away. It was a day like today, mixed in weather, swinging from mizzling rain to glorious sunshine. She was in a flowery dress and it moved well on her slender body. I can still see it and feel the rise it gave me.

I shock Rhonda into a guttural noise. I go on. My memories of Ella never fade for long.

She was the most beautiful creature. Even Cedric thought so. We climbed the tree on Dicey's Corner as we knew she'd pass under us and we could keep up our vigil of her unnoticed. We lay against the branches, and peered through the leaves quietly. Our pure thoughts were impure. I adored her.

Ella was about to be married even though she wasn't much older than us. She was a beautiful woman who was walking the road picking flowers. We were only boys and still she stirred the willies on us. I didn't know then that she'd always be the one for me, I just knew she was wonderful.

I stop and sniff. 'How time changes us handsome fellows into dirty old men?'

Rhonda merely smiles and lets us settle back into that day all those years ago.

We held our breath as she walked under the tree and her hair blew in the breeze. It was all golden and fair, like an angel's.

She is a cliché, a vision and was oh-so real then. Even now the sight of her in my mind's eye is very vivid.

On our way home, I made up my mind that I wanted to see her again. It took many months to know her patterns. I became what in today's world would be known as a stalker. To me, it was love and that is what it is to this day. I needed to be near her and this required a notebook and questioning of our neighbours. It began subtly at first and then was not so discreet.

It was known everywhere that I *had a notion* for Ella O'Brien.

That was nothing unusual. Most of the men thought her attractive. Whether married, single, widowed, or not that way inclined, most males understood, without it even having to be said, that Ella stirred us.

I doubt the women of today know what it is like to have nothing to enhance their beauty. With makeup, advertisements and photographs we are surrounded in fake prettiness. Ella was a living, natural beauty. She was like a walking work of art and, of course – Ella knew it.

Rhonda snorts. It doesn't stop me from talking.

Ella might have started out playing with my emotions. She toyed with men in general and we let her. It was a fun pastime for us all really.

Ella married young, and it was thought that she had picked well. She tricked a young doctoring student into making her pregnant and they'd lost the baby, but not the marriage. Dr O'Brien was a fine-looking chap. Even those of us not keen on mentioning the handsomeness in a man had to admit that he was a fine specimen. We all knew we couldn't compete with his brains either.

Ella had chosen a good man – or so we all presumed. Looking back, she too was floundering around from one great mistake to the next. We all felt she was plucked from a pedestal somewhere. Of course, she was a normal human and she made unholy blunders just like the rest of us idiots.

Most women loathed her. They were all jealous of her beauty, you see. Except her own doting relatives, of course. She had many relations and she was stifled by them and was rarely alone. I discovered that Ella's danders on a Sunday and her shopping trips were about the only times she was without companions. And one of her most frequent stops was in Daly's Butchers.

Jock Daly was a huge man, his hands were the size of shovels and his shoulders broad enough to carry sides of animals easily.

'I like your gumption, Charlie Quinn,' he said. 'Let's get you a trade.'

'Butchering?' Father hollered. The mere mention of working in the village sent him into a spin until he took all my wages. I managed to persuade Daly to slip me an odd sly shilling now and again, that Father knew nothing about. 'Surrounded in temptation!' was the usual shout as Father took my hard-earned crust. The time learning the trade flew in and I ignored the man as best I could. If only he knew how much temptation a then sixteen-year-old boy put in his own way. I always thought of ways to escape. I constantly dreamt of naked women and drinking porter. I became a good runner too. I moved quickly even with the big boots I wore to the butchers with the steel caps.

Cedric was to join what Father called the 'pagan newspaper men in Tyrone' and I was happy tearing across the fields and romping into Daly's a couple of minutes late every morning. Jock Daly didn't give out like usual folks. He would dig you in the ribs with his elbow and then grunt what it was for. It could be from a previous grievance of many days before and it hurt for many days after.

I was never late of a Tuesday. Never. That was the morning Ella O'Brien did her grocery shopping. In the early days, I wasn't allowed to take orders from the customers and I'd watch her from the back store. She'd nod and smile. I'd wait all week for that small grin where her lips were mine for a millisecond.

'Fine bit of meat,' Jock Daly would say at Ella and wink over at me. I stopped blushing as I wanted her to think I was a man. I wanted Ella to see me as the best man there ever was and I grew stronger, taller, fitter, fuller and learned how to speak proper.

Jock Daly was a talker and he could've sold sand to an Arab. He just had a way with him. I started to copy and mimic his methods. They didn't come easy to a shy, downtrodden youngster and Jock taught me how to pretend that I had the gift of the gab.

'You've a fire in that belly, young fella,' Jock would say. 'You'll go far, you know. Farther than any about here. Don't let the blood in you stop you from anything. You hear me now?'

I felt then if I could be a quarter the size and half the man of Jock Daly, I'd make something of myself for sure. He taught me everything about butchering and more importantly, he made me believe in my wink to charm the ladies.

'That flick of an eye will charm the pants off them,' Jock said. I was never usually praised and yes, I liked that kind of talk. I was a hot-blooded and frustrated boy. My whole life was hemmed in with the stone walls and the whispering about what was good and proper.

Thoughts of fleeing and tearing the clothes off women kept me living for most of my teenage years. I figured that kissing must be wild nice as people said that the films were all full of it. There was no other woman I wanted to kiss more than *my* Ella O'Brien. It never seemed to enter my stupidity that she was at least five years older and that she was not a moral option. It never occurred to me that she was married and out of my league. With a man like Jock hanging over my shoulder every day telling me how great I was at the job and what a charmer I was to the customers, I felt it was only a matter of time before I would grab and hold Ella O'Brien in my arms and press my mouth up against hers.

That's what kissing was then and it was all I thought about.

I lick my lips and close my eyes.

'Hullo, Charlie Quinn,' Ella said over the wooden counter past Jock.

My heart thumped like a drum. After years of her coming into Daly's I was shocked that she knew my name. The innocence.

'I'm looking for a nice bit of tongue,' she said and my resolve left.

Jock snorted and thumped my back hard. I nearly went through the counter. 'Give her what she's after, lad,' he said.

Ella knew how to torment us. There was no question that she enjoyed the teasing. She played games. I didn't know the joys of a woman's tongue and I didn't fully know then that she was goading me. How green was I?

Leaning against Rhonda's couch, I chuckle to myself, remembering a few times when she made me blush. I don't think badly of her. Even after all that's happened, she's still a pure goddess. I'm a sad old fool now and oh boy, back then, I was a pathetic young one.

'Lust is a strong force, Rhonda, and when they collide with love and mingle with morals, the explosion can be a devastating one.'

'Find a girl your own age, Charlie,' Jock ordered. Even though I knew he was right, those girls were easy prey. I was confident, had my own money, and a swagger of badness which my father failed to trounce out. I was marinaded with Jock's patter and pride. The combination of it all was a recipe for disaster. When I think of the glorious young skirts who made eyes as they passed Daly's door. All I did was scoff at them. I didn't even want to take advantage – it was all too easy. What is it they say, 'treat them mean and keep them keen?'

That worked. Ella O'Brien sure kept me keen. I would have done anything for her without wanting anything in return. When I thought of her the churning in my stomach stopped and the pains of anguish I felt disappeared. Thinking of her helps bring a normality. Despite all that happened, she's still good for my body.

That said, it possibly wasn't healthy in the long run. I became obsessive. She became a dream. I would still do anything for my Ella.

5

CHARLIE QUINN

R honda's child, Faye, has woken. She is playing with some teddies and we watch her together.

'They say thinking about the past is not good for a man. Maybe that's why I'm eaten away inside. When I think of Ella, I nearly always feel better. If I can ignore the guilt, she still brings me happiness.'

'When you say Ella O'Brien,' my biographer starts, 'do you mean *the* Ella O'Brien who's been in the papers again recently? She's in her eighties now? The one who's just come forward about her own story?'

'The very one.'

Is Rhonda disgusted or intrigued? It's hard to tell. Regardless, the dam has burst open and I must continue.

'Yes. That Ella O'Brien is my Ella.'

'You knew her? Before you left for Canada? You loved her when she was a young woman?'

'I did and I love her still.'

'And did you know of the recent interest in her?'

I sigh and clean my spectacles, giving myself a moment to compose my emotion.

'Is this why you've come home, Charlie? Is she the reason you've come back?' Rhonda asks, handing the child a sweet treat to silence her want of attention. 'Have you kept in touch with her over all these years?'

'If only I could have always been with her, things might have been different for us both.'

'I should let you continue, Charlie. Please, don't let my questions stop things. We're still recording.'

Talking through things, I gloss over months and years like they are easy to pass over. The work was tough and dealing with my father grew more and more difficult. After a year or more of working in Daly's, I moved out of home and into a small room in an old woman's terraced house in the centre of the village. I did odd jobs and kept her in meat in exchange for my bed and board. I was possibly around seventeen then and had my own few bob. I was no longer beholden to anyone else. I rarely saw Anna or Cedric and Jock's shop became my world as I waited to see my Ella every week.

Then she started coming in more often. Sometimes she would buy things she didn't normally purchase. Ella always waited until I could serve her. One day, I noticed the bruises on her wrist under a glove. She saw me glancing at them during the next visit too. It was when the black eye was obvious under the muck she tried to cover it with, that I became angry and mentioned it.

'It's nothing. I walked into the cupboard.'

Jock gripped my arm in the back store and hissed, 'Ignore the workings in another man's house. She's a flirt and a tease. The poor man's reputation is at stake and she pushes him to the edge of reason. You and I see her for a fleeting few minutes every week. We don't know what it is like to have to deal with that one every day! She'd drive any man to drink. Don't judge the poor sod of a doctor now. You don't know the whole story and only see one side of this mess.'

All I saw was another darling woman brutalised by a man who wanted control. Like my mother, Ella was the love of my life. She was all of the beauty I had in a grey world. Someone was hurting her as well. I was angry.

I stop for a sip of tea. Rhonda nods, urging me to go on. How can I tell her that I used all of that moral high ground and more to justify my lust and our sin? How can I tell her what I did?

I followed Ella one day. Finally, I gave in and stumbled after her in the street and cornered her in the back alley behind the pub. I think she knew that it was inevitable that we'd be together. She let me hold her wrist and remove the glove.

I kissed her bruised arm, then her eye and finally her lips.

Sighing now, I'm back to that first touching of our mouths. The press of warmth, the scent of perfume, the slick lipstick against cheek, the mound of her breast in my hand, the slide of Ella's glorious tongue between my teeth.

It's hard to describe the thrill of that kiss. That passion did everything. It shook me to the very boots. I'd no idea that men and women mingled tongues and the naughtiness was too wonderful. It felt like a daydream until there was a batter of a beer barrel in the yard near us and a scuffle of the gate being opened. We both ran from the spot like children. She flittered away in one direction and I raced in the other. I found it hard to move with a large horn between my legs.

Rhonda chuckles.

I am reminded of Ella's giggle when I got a sneaky note into her basket. She also managed a first visit to the room in my lodgings. I smuggled her in when the October twilight gave way to clandestine seductions. It was more than sex. To me it was a divine time.

I was like a blind stallion and we were both walking into

disaster. I cared little for the consequences. I never thought of us being caught and she didn't seem in the least bit scared.

She must've been petrified as she took a great risk to sneak away from her husband, and prying family, and cycle the few miles into town. She must've trusted me to never speak of it to anyone.

'I cannot believe it,' I told her over and over when finally she was in the ramshackle room with its peeling wallpaper and damp ceiling. 'Why have you agreed to come here?'

'I need you to make love to me, Charlie,' Ella said without even blushing.

I start to cough and stop my ramblings. Holding my painful side and hip I try to gather myself. The room is warm and I heave at my tight shirt collar with a trembling finger.

Rhonda smirks. There's a quick flash of understanding between us that we're reaching the time when a film closes the bedroom door or a programme goes to commercial break. 'Please go on, Charlie. Tell it to me the way that it was. It's okay.'

She looks at her notebook and shuffles her bum on the seat.

'I'll try,' I say and open a button near the top of my shirt. Things cool slightly and I begin again.

I had fantasised non-stop about how she would have looked naked. Every man in Tyrone thought about it. You see, there were no images of naked women in those days. I had imaginings of the curves but there was little else to educate me.

We were alone. Ella took the lead and walked me onto the bed. She sat and removed my trousers. Then, without much hesitation she stripped bare while I held my cock in my hand and lost my mind in the sight of her.

I wasn't sure that I'd know what to do. I had only listened to Jock or seen the dogs at it in the street. I had grown up from that boy in the tree but I was still a naive seventeen-year-old fella with some bulging muscles and notions. I knew very little about a woman's needs. It was a very nice surprise when I discovered what their bodies did to us.

Ella showed me what her mouth could do. I thought I'd burst with longing. She let me lie on her, and slide between her legs and find the hidden place. We became one that evening. I filled my Ella with seeds of love and promised to always be hers. It was unbelievable. I don't think I've ever made love like it since. It lasted no time at all. I was a fumbling wreck and she was always glancing at the door, which wouldn't lock.

It was possibly the best time of my life with a woman. My first and best time.

Of course, Ella returned to my room again. For a few months, it was almost weekly. Each time we got more brazen, more lost in each other's bodies, more entangled in the nakedness. The seduction of each other's souls was even more intense. I made her shudder with desire and she made me moan loudly. It was the type of passion I always think of when I want... It was perfection.

We were sinners and we were in love. Desperately, I clung to her when she wanted to leave. When she had to go I hugged into her even more. I saw it as desertion. The aroma of Ella lingered in the bed sheets and I'd sniff them until she returned to give herself to me again.

I sucked every part of her, caressed each inch of skin with lips and loved every hair, every mole, rubbed deep inside her and devoured my Ella with lust. In between our sessions of love-making, I pulled my penis raw and never stopped thinking about how I might get inside her the next time. Which angle might get me deeper, longer, or stronger. I longed to make her gasp in pleasure. I loved to see her bite her bottom lip, and to hear her moan when I pumped with eager hips.

As a young fellow, I had stamina for such things. She must've been delighted with my enthusiasm. I could see why men wanted women all to themselves and why married beds were sacred places. My mattress became an altar to Ella and I'd have done anything to have taken her all day every day into those blankets. I urged her to stay for more than a fleeting few hours. I couldn't think of Ella doing those things with a husband or someone else, and every now and again I asked things which must have hurt her.

'Do you let other men do this? Does your husband do it?'

'No,' she always answered and in my youthful innocence I believed that. In her defence, I feel she was truthful as really I've never been with any other woman in the way I was with my Ella.

6

RHONDA QUINN

As I go about the mundane household chores that somehow have all become my job, I cannot help envying this Ella O'Brien. That is some turn-up for the books. Ella has lingered in the nation's consciousness for decades. As much as her name is muck, and she's accused of all sorts, a man has loved her passionately for more than sixty years. Charlie talks of her with such desire I thump the washing into the machine and slam the door shut.

Joe returns home, kicks the door closed, tosses his things on the newly-washed hall tiles and sits with the whisky I've poured for him. He'll swirl it annoyingly and wait on his dinner. There's no kiss, no lingering embrace.

'How did today go?' he asks. He has joined me by the sink while I peel the potatoes. He didn't check on Faye, didn't notice her and those dollies she thumps all over the house.

'Fine. Today was fine.' I don't look at him.

'Do you still like the old boy? Or is he in the doghouse too?'

I stop peeling and think for a second.

'I'll take that as a no then. You think we're both bastards.'

'You're only home. Can you at least try and be glad to see me and your daughter? You're more interested in that old codger.'

Joe has a knack of making me feel as if I'm being annoyed about nothing as usual. Like I'm being a bitch.

Joe reaches out to touch my shoulder. He doesn't reach it and retreats back to the table. He picks at the side of the bread I've baked. 'Is Charlie sleeping? I'm almost afraid to speak.' Eating, he says, 'Yum. This bread looks good. You're getting good at the baking.'

I slap the lid on the saucepan for the potatoes and check on Faye out of the corner of my eye. For two, she's exceptionally good. I'm grateful that she can self-soothe. She's learning all the time to play by herself and she's mostly quiet and placid. I'm blessed and I don't always feel it.

'He's back in Ireland because of *that* Ella O'Brien. It's nothing to do with wanting to connect with his own family. It's all to do with the scandal,' I announce.

Joe is mid-sip and his eyes widen.

'I know. He just admitted he was a lover of hers. I'm not sure what to make of it.'

'Shit!'

'And he knew her from before all this madness started. He's been in love with her all this time.'

'You were right. You can smell a story coming! Holy God!'

I don't want to be smug and say I told you so. Instead, I bite my lip and add, 'I'm not sure I'm comfortable with all of it. That Ella is one evil cow – we all know that. And he's making out that she's some sort of beautiful saint. Who will want to hear about him and the likes of her?'

'Everyone will. You know yourself that since that news down the country, Ella's back in the papers. There's a fascination about her. This is going to be big. Charlie knows it too. Isn't he a dark horse? Her lover, eh? Clever Charlie!'

'Mum will explode about this. You know how she hates it when people go on about Ella O'Brien. If she gets a notion that Charlie is going to connect this family with that filth, you can imagine her reaction.'

'Filth is a bit strong, Ronnie.'

'Is it?'

Faye toddles over, uncertain of our mood and of her feet. She holds a doll out to Joe and he takes it. 'I know it's hard to imagine what that woman did. Charlie must have somethin' to say. He's in pain. You can tell and he's come all this way, after all this time. He must want to finally be at peace with whatever he knows.'

Watching Joe lift Faye into his arms, I wonder what way he sees me. Would he speak of our love in the way Charlie does about Ella? I often wonder does Joe regret leaving that woman he was with. He was almost engaged when we met. He might regret his choice.

'We'll have to keep all of this to ourselves for now,' I say softly as I can hear Charlie in the hallway.

'I know to tell your mother sweet feck all,' Joe says and chuckles. He kisses Faye's cheek and whispers, 'At least he's given us something to talk about.' Joe looks expectantly at me. He wants to kiss. I don't want to. Automatically it happens. The smack of mouths is functional and Faye clashes the dolly upwards and catches me on the nose.

I squeal and move backwards, knocking over the saucepan of potatoes. Water pours down the cooker, worktops and drips down the cupboard doors. Faye howls, knowing she's hurt someone and Joe tries to silence us both. The sting eases. I don't want to give in that it wasn't quite as bad as it seems. Holding my nose, I leave Joe to a screaming toddler and streaming water. Charlie meets me in the hallway and in true Charlie style, ignores the drama and toddles on up the hall.

I sink into our bed, fully clothed. Turning in to the pillow, I gurgle out a silent cry. Joe will tell Charlie about what happened and make me out to be another hysterical woman. Charlie will roll his eyes and agree with him.

Looking at the ceiling, I think about my own hidden secrets. Who am I to judge Charlie Quinn?

7

CHARLIE QUINN

Rhonda has made tea and switched on the lamps on the side tables littering the corners of their fine, modern sitting room. She's turned on the tape recorder and the child has had a nappy change and we've not spoken for maybe thirty minutes.

Rhonda's husband is making us all supper in the kitchen and Faye's sucking on another plastic contraption. She's nestled into her mother's arms. It pains me to think of what might have been for Ella and I. We would have lived like this. It would have been possible.

'Are you disgusted with my chatter?' I ask Rhonda. 'I just want to show you that our time was precious. It was beautiful.'

'Of course I don't mind you talking like this, Charlie. It's your life, your feelings, your story,' Rhonda answers. 'We all know what it is like to be in love. You describe it beautifully. It must exhaust you though?' I don't answer, and she adds, 'You've a wonderful voice and I feel you need to tell this now.'

'Can I go back? Can I go on?'

'Yes, of course.'

The weather was bad for weeks. Rain and wind heaped

down like it was angry with us. I wanted to enjoy a walk with Ella on the road I first saw her on. I thought maybe we could cavort in the fields in the sun – it wasn't to be. December brought frosty evenings and there was little chance of Ella visiting and spending a few minutes naked with me. I was very sad.

Jock's talk was always about travelling then. He made it sound like a big adventure. He rambled on about the ships going across the oceans to new worlds. 'If I was a young fella like you, Charlie, I'd be away. You've a trade behind you and I can get you sorted. Canada is a big country. Why not think of it? You'd be far gone to the lands of plenty. Living a life the rest of us can only dream of. Mind you, I don't want you to go. Ach, it would be the best thing. You have to spread those wings and be gone from here, my boy. There's nothing to keep you. Get you gone.'

Did he know and sense the disaster and try to warn me off? There was nowhere I could go without Ella and for a long time I couldn't even get to tell her that I might try to take her across the waves.

It's hard to describe the stifled life we led then. The way people lived in each other's pockets. The newspapers and the picture houses brought the outside world to us. It all was just out of reach. Even when we saw Shirley Temple and the likes, there was little point in dreaming of riches, wide-open spaces and adventure, when all the butchering needed done and the rain poured down the same old street.

America started to descend into the Great Depression. The Irish didn't really notice and I turned eighteen. It was Jock who caused a fuss and got his wife to ask me to dinner. She made a cake the following weekend. Childless Jock might've thought of me as his own then, but his wife was not fond of Charlie Quinn. I was full of cheek and probably known to be a womaniser of unobtainable women. She was kind that evening and wished me a good birthday and future.

I was grateful for that.

Jock and I went to the pub on the way back to my lodgings. I got drunk, of course, and on the way home, I cried into his shoulder about my Ella.

I don't know what exactly I confessed to that night, there wasn't any more said about it. The next day went on as before and as my head thumped I forgot about it. He treated me no differently and all was fine until the Tuesday morning.

'Put an end to it, boy,' Jock hissed, grabbing my arm hard before Ella's usual time in the butcher's. 'She's messing your head and heart. Trust me. I'm telling you there is to be no more of it. End this – Now!'

Ella sauntered in, bringing the sun and she knocked the rain off her scarf. Jock grunted his greeting and somehow she knew instantly that I had let her down. She took to her heels without the sausages and kidneys. Racing after her, I could hear Jock's voice calling, 'Have sense now, young fella. Have sense.'

Everyone was watching as I caught up with her. The few people on the street were all delighted to witness something of note in the village.

'Leave me be,' Ella stammered, peering around us at the watchful eyes. 'You're making a spectacle.'

'Come back into the shop and get your sausages,' I said confidently.

'I know that beast, Jock, knows something he shouldn't?' Her beauty was on fire with fear.

'I got drunk. It was my birthday. I was upset. He knows nothing much. Just that... I love you.'

Ella's lips parted to spit out a lashing of annoyance. It would have been a different lashing than what I was used to. She stopped and took my arm and pulled me in close. I could smell her scent, the perfume she wore or the face cream that smelt good enough to eat. 'Don't be a silly boy.'

When a man professes his love and gets called a silly boy in the middle of a busy village street, it does nothing for the confidence or the mood.

I got angry. 'I can see now why he thumps you. My hand is itching. You need a good slap.'

It was a terrible thing to say. Even to this day after all the worst things I've done in life, that sentence sticks in the craw. It tore down between us like a knife through a carcase.

8

CHARLIE QUINN

Our fall out didn't stop Ella coming into the butcher's for meat. It couldn't or the whole place would be sure that we were at something. It was early 1930 and women, like now, were always the ones to blame for a man's sexual desires. I was a mere child or a lovesick boy and she was a woman of the world. She planned and executed her seduction, and I was a more than willing accomplice in the immoral crimes.

Jock was happy. 'Good lad, I'm glad that you had the sense to end it.'

'I was silly to think she was mine. She's a fine woman. A nice woman and I'm a silly boy. She never... we never. I dreamt it all up. She's a good woman and I have a good imagination.'

Those words grated and that lie was almost tougher than any other. Jock let on that he believed it. I went on to try and make it all look like nothing more than an infatuation. At times I even convinced myself that she'd never been in the bed I could still smell her in.

For weeks it was all terrible until there was a tiny knock on the back window of my lodgings. The evening was fair for January and in the moonlight she was like a ghost, an illicit presence from another time and place. Saying nothing, we were one before I had time to even grasp that she was back.

'Sorry,' she murmured as I took her over and over on the squeaking mattress and the flopping frame. 'I was afraid.'

'Don't be sorry. It was me,' the silly boy said and wiped her tears away from those rosy cheeks. 'Come away with me. Let's leave here. Let's go to Canada. America, anywhere. Say you'll come.'

'Yes,' she agreed and we plotted out plans amid the orgasms. We were insatiable, lost in rampant fantasies of the future.

'I can't go. Not really. I'm married, Charlie. You forget that.' She said that more than once and I didn't care about it.

Now, that seems ridiculous. I was a slip of a lad and Ella was a curvy woman with breasts like mountains and legs that were heavenly. She was unsullied by lines or wrinkles and the smoothness of her thighs and buttocks is something I can still feel. It was more than love. As you can hear, I was horny for Ella, an animal in my desires. I wasn't alone, she liked sex as much as I did.

'You'll change. You'll want me demure and plain,' she said. 'You'll want your dinner on the table and want me pregnant and waiting on you at home. I'll be supposed to be meek and mild.'

The images she described were nice. A woman stayed at home then. Once married there was no chance she'd be allowed to work. That's the way things were and in my youth I failed to understand why she felt trapped by such things.

'Being away from here will change your life and it won't change mine,' Ella said. 'You see life as a big man's adventure. A woman's lot will always be the same no matter where she goes. I'll always be stuck.'

I couldn't get to grips with all of her preaching in those days. I tried to.

'I'll have to be a butcher wherever we go. I know what you

mean. I'll have to use it to make us money. I don't like it much. You've no trade but I'll make enough for us both. You're not to worry. We'll be fine.'

She leaned back against the pillows then and rounded her belly with that slender hand and stopped the world with the words, 'And can you care for a child that neither of us want?'

It took me many minutes to hear it clearly and process the meaning. I'm not sure I ever fully understood that sentence.

'Baby?' I think I asked.

'It might be yours. It might not.'

It had occurred to me that she humped with her husband and the uncertainty in those words were terribly sore. I'm sure I lit a cigarette then.

'That shut up your plans!' She had a cruel tone at times and there it was again.

'It's a shock, that's all.'

I know that many men would have left her then. She expected that. Of course, I doubted if Ella ever truly loved me. I've imagined that she was a bad woman. Perhaps these things are true. Maybe I was just a bit of rough for her? I've found that I was that for a few women over the years. No, I don't like to think that I was that. I wanted to be Ella's one true love, like she was mine. I was sure that she never lied to me, and I felt she was good for me. Those thoughts always return.

She sat up tall and said, 'My husband knows about the baby and thinks it's his. Life will be better that way.'

Of course, a married woman should and would want her husband's baby. In a normal world that would be the right thing, it was like a furnace burning away all decency.

'It's mine!' I shouted as she tried to silence the anger. Like a child myself, our baby was a possession, a toy. 'Mine! It's mine.'

'Look around you, Charlie. You can't care for a wife and child.'

She was right. I had nothing. Came from nothing. Knew nothing. She would never be totally mine. I could barely breathe. I didn't want to cry or beg – I did both.

'Why?' I sobbed. 'Why have you done this?'

I failed to realise that I had done something wrong too.

'I'm sorry,' she whispered into my sodden cheek and as the door clicked closed I listened for those footsteps that took her silently away. I heard nothing more and she was gone.

9

CHARLIE QUINN

The turmoil was fierce. Every possible scenario raced in and out, tossing me into despair. It was possibly only a week until Ella returned in the dead of night.

Frozen from the wintery air she slunk under the covers and we got lost for a while. Lying in those slender arms felt like the most natural place to be and nothing was wrong with the movie screen playing for us alone.

Stopping now, I take a long look at Rhonda. She is listening intently and I don't want to lie – yet it might be just my own version of things. To this very day there's a struggle with the truth.

'You're doing well,' Rhonda says as encouragement. 'I know this is hard. You were telling me about having no one to listen to you. I'm here now, Charlie. Tell me all of it.'

I take a deep breath and return to our bed.

'It's going to be all right,' Ella promised. 'We might make it to a boat. Can we afford two tickets? Do you have savings?'

Faced with the reality of it shocked me into silence. She sensed the wariness and decided to dress herself. She was leaving again and that was not good and physically I was weak with it all.

'Are we really going to run away together?' she asked, or I may have suggested it as I thought about little else.

'I don't want this child and I might lose it anyhow. I tend not to keep them. If it's yours it might be stronger though and we need to be prepared for that.'

I wasn't sure I even knew where babies grew in a woman. I knew they got bigger. I wasn't altogether sure if women had wombs like the animals I butchered. Also, I worried about the poking I did into Ella but she still seemed to like it. That was the limit of my understanding and other than she was married to a doctor, that was possibly all she knew too.

'What if the doctor finds out?' I know I asked. 'What will he do?'

'He won't. If he does, he could kill me. At the very least he'd batter me senseless and then kick me out. I couldn't go to my family. They'd be disgraced. I'm risking everything to be with you, Charlie. You do know that?'

I knew the gossips and the tight-knit community would shun us both for the sinning. I hadn't enough stashed in the mattress to take us anywhere. Anyhow, I'd never travelled farther than the capital and even that had been when I was a small child. Mammy had been running away then too. We'd gone to stay with a rich relative of hers. It hadn't lasted long as Father had come and dragged us all home. Life has that way of forcing you back down to the place you belong.

'I know that it's dangerous. Of course I do. I just know that I love you and we must make plans to get far away from here,' I told her.

'I look old enough to be your mother. Can you at least grow some facial hair?'

'What kind of talk is that? You're only a few years older. Don't be a mean cow. I'm a fine man.'

She giggled. Beautiful Ella always made me smile. Even in the darkest of nights and days, she was a lighthouse.

'The baby?' I asked, touching her rounded belly. 'When you say you don't want it, what do you mean?'

'I lose them. They eventually bleed out of me. I cannot love it until it becomes a child. Otherwise I'd go mad. I used to think that he hurt them with some of the battering he does at me. I believe the babies know that they have no safe home and leave.'

She wasn't sad in saying that. It came out matter-of-fact. Losing babies had become normal and perhaps it was. Women suffered terribly in those days and it wasn't talked about. It seems wrong that a good woman must endure pain in silence over and over and have to become numb to it all.

'It's mine. It'll grow strong – like me. Isn't that right?' I said at the growing tummy mound. She held me close and agreed.

Did I really want a baby to come? I was not long eighteen. I had no idea of the work or responsibility. The baby was our love and I was sure it cemented us together somehow. If it was mine I'd have one up on the bastard husband who hurt Ella. The baby gave us a bigger reason to escape. That meant I wanted it more than anything. I never understood then that the baby was a real person. To me, it was a ray of hope, an intangible prospect – a future with Ella.

Rhonda reaches for her recorder, the movement of her in my eyeline stirs the past into the present. It is late and she looks as tired as I feel. 'It's still recording,' she tells me and looks at her watch. 'Charlie, you must be exhausted altogether now?'

'I am. It's tiring remembering.'

'Before we go to sleep, Charlie, can I ask you something? Is this baby that you're talking about... is this child the one that started all of the trouble?'

10

RHONDA IRWIN

I'm not sleeping. The drifting into oblivion doesn't happen despite the tiredness. Without sleep I'm more snarky than usual.

'He got Ella pregnant,' I tell Joe as he comes from his morning shower. Joe still looks good. There's no extra pregnancy weight on him. The towel drops and he wipes the excess moisture from his groin while thinking about what I've said. 'Did you hear me? One of her babies was Charlie's?'

'I'm still trying to wake up, don't shout.'

'When else do I get a chance to tell you things? I'm not shouting.'

'Don't lose your temper with me about it. You should have known. As soon as he mentioned them being lovers it makes sense that he knew about the babies.'

'He looked sick yesterday. He says that he's fine, that he may be dying – but he's fine. I feel guilty all the time having him here. I'm exploiting a sick man.'

Joe sits on the end of the bed. I still find him attractive. More than that actually, I want him to find me irresistible despite my bedhead and old nightdress.

'He said to me the other day that he wants it to be between you both for now. I don't think you should tell me anymore. It might not help things.'

'Why doesn't he want you to know?' My voice is high-pitched.

'Said my opinion matters to him.' Joe swipes the towel across his hair.

'And mine doesn't?' I sit up in the bed. 'He doesn't care what I think?'

'He's a man's man. Spent much of his life with the cowboys,' Joe rationalises – another slight towards me as if it was nothing. 'He said that he's not used to worrying about women's opinions because they usually love him. I told him that you don't like anyone lately. He disagreed and said that he thinks you're kinder than many would be with him.'

'I'm not a softie.'

'I know that.' Joe smiles and pulls on his underwear. 'In fairness, you're good with Charlie. It's nice to see.'

'Are you saying that I'm not nice with you?'

'Don't twist this, Ronnie. We're talking about what's happening. Don't fight. I'm too tired to start this first thing.'

I have to agree and nod. 'I didn't sleep much. I'm going to contact some people today. Make enquiries. Do some research. I've many questions and he refuses to let me ask them.'

'Charlie is used to getting his own way.'

'What does he want from all of this?' I ask myself as much as Joe. 'What is it all about?'

Joe shrugs. 'Maybe he wants to help Ella in some way. If he still loves her. He might want to show another side to the story. Share something to make things better.'

'I doubt there's much that could help *that* one. And, after sixty years, what difference would it make now?'

As Joe ties a large knot in his tie, and fixes his collar, I recall when we met. I'd neatened his tie. 'Would you want to help me after that long?' I say. He's pulling on his jacket and doesn't fully hear me.

'What did ya say?' he asks, straightening his shirt and making sure it's tucked in, as he buckles his belt. 'And, I think you're enjoying this, even though you don't want to admit it. You're getting as much from this as he is and no, you're not using him. He's helping you.'

'Why do you say that?'

'It's given you a focus. You're speaking and thinking about writing again.' Those lovely eyes of Joe's need me to agree. He has spent a long time worried. I'm not sure whether that's been for his own selfish reasons or out of love for us. 'Do you still like him?' Joe asks. 'He thinks he's a real ladies' man. Charlie is sure that you like him.'

'Is he now?'

'Yup. Told me that you find him fascinating and that you find me boring.'

I'm out of the bed with a jolt.

'He's probably astute enough,' Joe says, finding his shoes and dragging one on. He sits on the end of the bed to settle a foot into the other shoe and ties both laces. 'He knows you're finding motherhood tough. And before you kill me – we both are finding being parents very difficult. When you live with us it is bound to be obvious. What with us being forced together and whatnot, it's not as easy as we both thought. Charlie sees that. Don't look at me like that. Most people are the same. They just don't talk about it.'

'I don't find you boring,' I say, feeling unattractive beside Joe's fully-clothed frame. 'I only find our life tedious. God, you're right, it's too early for these conversations.'

'Faye will be up soon and you're going to have a full-on day. I know that I escape every day.' Joe curls me into those arms, and

I'm grateful. He smells familiar and safe. For once he is really seeing me and our situation. There's the traditional rub of my arse and the nuzzle into my neck. 'I gotta go,' Joe mutters, leaving my arms. He whispers while opening the door, 'Don't be like Ella O'Brien and kill anyone while I'm away.'

It closes with a click. I slump onto the bed. He was trying to be funny. It wasn't. I take it that he sees me as a deranged, irrational woman. Faye's morning whimper starts from the other room and I pull a pillow over my head.

11

CHARLIE QUINN

The morning brings me back to Rhonda's sofa, watching Faye at play. There's an aroma of coffee and the nice sights of their family life. I have confided in this stranger when her man has gone to work or left us alone. No doubt they both are worried. They may have been having night-time whisperings about the can of worms they've opened.

'The media frenzy about Ella O'Brien made me stay awake last night,' Rhonda says, a hint of worry in her voice. 'Does Ella know that you are in Ireland, Charlie? Does she know that you are still alive? Have you made contact with her at all?'

I shrug and wipe a tear from the wrinkle in my cheek.

'Should I help you reach her?'

The emotion chokes me and, stumbling to rise, I fail to reach the kitchen sink. Vomit spews and startles us all. The projectile mess is upsetting and foul-smelling. Rhonda links me back to a soft spot on a chair and produces a basin and plops down a cup of tea with directions of use and platitudes of, 'Don't worry now. Let's get you right. Did you take your medications?'

'Sorry,' is all I manage as she mops and cleans. The waft of bleach doesn't help my heaving stomach.

'A mother is well-used to vomit, Charlie. All is fine now. Are you all right?'

Nodding, I lie to her. 'I've never been okay, you know. Never. I've always been a bad brute.'

'Nonsense!'

Despite the weakness I know I need to tell all of it. Every bad step, each awful choice – regardless of what Rhonda thinks. Like a Catholic at confessional, I'm here for a purpose. I always envied their offloading of a lifetime of sin and anguish. It seems unfair to burden her. Rhonda is a journalist though and might be able to place it somewhere for her own gain. Don't papers pay for people's souls to be read?

I motion a hand towards the recorder and she nods that we are ready for the work ahead. Faye's eyes don't follow me anymore. Thankfully, she is lost in the innocent world of teddies and teacups.

'I came back here and I'm not totally sure why,' I admit.

'You love Ella,' Rhonda says.

I nod, wondering how much clever Rhonda is piecing together correctly.

'One of Ella's babies was yours, Charlie? I was trying to work out the timescales...'

Closing out the present, I see Ella on the mattress with the swell of my baby inside her. I can touch that smooth, soft skin and smile into those beaming eyes. It was my baby and I rubbed her tummy and talked to what belonged to me inside.

The baby kept the churning of my innards calm and the presence of Ella in my room took all pain away. Ella glowed and was finally enjoying the pregnancy. She talked about feeling happy and content. We made plans and gathered money together into a large jar.

In my ignorance I didn't even think to ask how long we had before the baby would come. I suppose I knew vaguely it would be a few more months of just the two of us. Ella grew larger. Her beauty intensified and our lovemaking was ecstasy. I was lost, living in a haze, childlike in my expectations and understanding of what was happening.

It was a Friday when the gossip reached Daly's. I'm not sure who said it first or how I heard the words.

'Ella O'Brien has been carted off in broad daylight. The poor baby born early again and she's accused of killing it. Might she have murdered the others too?'

Jock's expression was shocked as he filled the order for sausages. I can still see him swing them, cut them and package them, his eyes never leaving mine.

'You were missing earlier. What do you know about this? You need away, boy. Today, you need gone!' Jock hauled me into the cold store. 'Listen to me now. Nothing good will come of you being here when the shit flies into the air. You hear me?'

The shaking he did brought me around somewhat.

'Sounds like the baby is gone and she's in bother. That husband and his family will make her hang. Monied bastards won't lie down under this. If there's even a whiff of what you two have been at, there'll be hell to pay. Someone is bound to know. They'll crucify you too.'

'She didn't murder our baby,' I whispered. 'This one is mine and she was happy and it was strong. I felt it move and...'

Jock's grip was firm and his voice was tired and afraid. 'It's all a misunderstanding then. She'll not look any better with a snivelling boy mentioning feeling his baby inside her. There's always been talk about Ella being a bad egg. We all know that. She'll not come off any better with an eighteen-year-old lover telling all and sundry that this is his baby! Don't you see you have to go now, Charlie? You gotta escape for her sake and yours. One of you in trouble is more than enough.'

The brandy and the cold air in the store brought me around

some more and Jock's words did have a ring of truth in them. We'd talked about the family surrounding her on both sides. One as controlling as the other was dangerous. Her in-laws were lawyers; educated, religious zealots, almost as bad as my own father. We had a similarity in the trapped natures of our existences. Our dreams of escaping were matched over and over in the whispers in the dark.

'I can't leave her,' I muttered. On that sad day, in my heart of hearts, I was more scared than in love. Even a rebel like me sensed that I was no match for the realities caving in. 'Where is she?' I asked and Jock went to the public house to see what the news was. I served customers, waiting for them to mention my Ella. I was afraid to ask about the gossip in case I started to cry or gave myself away.

Jock's news was terrible. 'Arrested for infanticide. That means killing children to you and me. Three counts of it and the husband ranting and raving that she's evil. There's no talk of you. Before she lets something slip or that husband finds out, you must get yourself off on a boat. I'll arrange it.'

'Where?' I asked, meaning where Ella was but Jock's tale went into the blood found in their own home and the state Ella was found in alone with another dead infant. The details were sordid, horrid and graphic, the usual Irish garishness not lost in the sadness of it all.

'She's off with the authorities, God knows where and I for one am not sorry to see her go.' Jock thought Ella guilty too. No amount of pleading would change that. I saw it in his face, the cut of his shoulders and the stance of him in the doorway. 'Time you knew that her beauty is a mask for something awful. She bewitched you. It's time now to strike out from here and forget all of this bad business. You must go before anyone suspects and hauls you in as an accomplice and a cuckolding blaggard. That bitch knew what she was doing all along, seducing you and then doing away with the precious little thing because it looks nothing like she wanted.'

He went on to describe the baby. A girl with a shock of red hair and pale skin, and adding for dramatic effect that the last child of Ella's found dead had been dark-skinned.

'The poor creature almost as dark as your boot when found in Ella's arms in the back alley of the public house.'

That was explained away by her doctoring husband as "the unusual colour from the difficult birthing situation and lack of air". According to Jock everyone surmised that Ella had taken up with the black labouring man who passed through that summer. This was all new information to me and it filtered in slowly and hurt like hell.

'Your hair isn't red,' Jock shouted, startling me out of the images of Ella with the nice, muscled, black man who'd greeted everyone when passing in the street. 'She wasn't true to you either. Are you listening?'

My mother's hair had tinges of red through it and I failed to speak of it to Jock. He bundled me and my trembling up and almost carried me to the lodging house to pack.

'I'm sending you to that cousin of mine in Canada. He'll get you started and get you on your feet. You need gone from here as soon as possible.'

I don't want to look at Rhonda or see her disgust. Instead, I reach for the cold teacup, stick my nose inside it and squeeze my eyelids together, blocking out the swirling images. Some of them I can tell her now, others I must leave alone.

There were not many protests about leaving.

If I could ask Jock (who is long gone now) to set my mind at ease I would. I want to know what I said and did then. I remember very little of the decisions. I doubt I was gallant or courageous. There was only the sense of abandonment, fear and the total disappointment. I believed for that period of time that

Ella was somehow to blame for it all. That suited the coward, Charlie Quinn.

But, in my heart, too, I loved her enough to know it wasn't her fault. The survivalist instinct that I've always harboured took over. I can see myself running in those steel-capped boots up the gangway to the largest ship I'd ever seen.

I chance a look at Rhonda now as blackness invades the daylight. 'If you were Ella O'Brien, would you want to see me?' I ask her.

12

CHARLIE QUINN

In the morning I cannot move from this soft, new-fangled mattress. The room is a small one for guests and the stuffiness and closeted air is all that gets my feet to the floor. I need out.

I've slept too long and much of the morning is gone. I refuse breakfast and take coffee. Watching Rhonda make us what she calls 'some brunchtime soup', I cannot help wondering what she's thinking. What must she make of the storm surrounding Ella now? As a mother she'll have thoughts I won't have. Times change. The thinking around children out of wedlock is slightly different in 1990. The twists and turns of publicity will flavour Rhonda's understanding of Ella's journey too. What a mess!

There's a new interest in the minds of criminals – a fashion for psychology and analysing, judging and making decisions about what must have happened. Those accused of murdering their own children are still outside this scope. They are taboo. People take sides on conspiracies. Everyone is sure about what must have happened. They don't know the secrets. Until people speak out, we never really know the truth – end of story.

When Ella was arrested, Ireland went into a state of shock.

We all did. The whole world at one time or another seems to have an opinion on what happened to Ella's babies. The father's role was uninteresting or not spoken about. The only intriguing element is that of the mother's state of mind or morals. A mother killing her own child is something off the scale of reason. There's nothing worse.

To this day I scream inside about the suffering Ella endured. She must have coped with many things for years before and after this incident. And my Ella is not considered as a real person. As a woman is not truly thought of, unless it is to condemn her.

'What do you believe about it all?' I ask Rhonda's back. Her shoulders tense immediately on the question and I hear her sigh into a silence.

'You are like them all. You think that there is no smoke without fire. You think she's a bad woman,' I say.

'You weren't there, were you, Charlie? You cannot know either.'

'I know more than most. I need to tell you all of it. I might have saved them both. I am a bad, bad man.'

'Would you not go to her now, Charlie? Should you not try to talk with her? Go and see her?'

'I'm a coward. I need to sort things in my own head and heart first. Can you help me do that?' I plead.

Rhonda nods and stirs again at the saucepan. 'Still, I think you should contact her. She's an elderly woman and you're not well. Between you both there might be some closure, some healing if you could see and talk to one another?'

'Not until you know more. Then you can tell me how you feel. You can say, as a woman, how Ella might feel about seeing me.'

'Okay, we cannot waste time as really this needs sorted as soon as possible.'

'It's been over sixty years. A few more days here or there isn't going to make any difference.' I look out into their garden. 'Ella won't want to see me after all this time in convents and asylums. She's not going to be the same person. She'll not have the same feelings. Just like I'm changed beyond recognition. I'm not that young boy who left Ireland all those years ago.'

'You make out that you're a bad man, Charlie. From what you told me, you weren't to blame. What could you have done? Jock was right. If you came forward, it would have made things worse. He was a good friend to you.'

'Was he now?' I say through gritted teeth. 'I have cursed him almost every day for the last sixty years. Ella probably spent her life doing the same about me. That's the real cancer, and the cure won't come when I see or speak to her. I fear it will kill me altogether.'

'Ella has promised to end the mystery we've all been curious about. She's finally going to speak about that time. She is going to want to know that you are here to back up her side of things. I'm sure that's what she'll hope for.'

'How do you know that I will do right by her?'

Rhonda stops stirring.

'I only know what a young boy believed and what an old man can recall. It might not match her version,' I admit. 'What then? Will I just open more old wounds? I've learned from experience that when I talk it usually makes things worse. I think I'll wait and see what Ella has to say first. Is that cruel?'

'Maybe. Maybe not. It makes sense to see what she says and what the public think of her revelations. It's been a long time and she might have kept many secrets from you, too, Charlie. You need to protect yourself. I understand that.'

'I don't want to hide,' I admit loudly and cough. 'I'm just afraid of making things worse for Ella. There's no point in coming all of this way, after all of this time, and making things worse.' Reaching into my pocket I pull out my passport and hand it to Rhonda.

She takes it and opens the document, reading the name and comparing me to the old photograph.

'Who is this?' Rhonda asks, squinting at both me and the document in her hand. 'Why do you have a fake passport, Charlie?'

'You see. Ella might need a better knight in shining armour. The Charlie Quinn you all know and the one who loved Ella is a wanted man. I may even be a worse criminal than twenty Ella O'Briens.'

13

RHONDA IRWIN

There is a criminal sitting in my kitchen. I use Faye's nappy as an excuse to move from dealing with him. Just when I was starting to overlook his social quietness as an oddity, a like-able quirk and I was becoming used to his wonderful ramblings about love and life in the past – he jerks me into reality.

What the hell is happening to my life? There's a fugitive of some kind sitting in our house. Sleeping contentedly and snoring loudly in our orbit for days now. I invited him in and have been enabling him!

Since he arrived, our family have talked to and fro about Charlie and there was never any doubt that he was this long-lost relation. Why would anyone reappear after sixty years and pretend to be an ordinary fellow with no living relatives or inheritance to claim?

Now that man in the kitchen could be lying about being our Charlie Quinn. He claims to be someone else entirely. People recognised him immediately though. I lift my mobile to ring Joe. What is the point of that, what do I say?

My mother will have a fit about what he might drag up. I thought it might just be the scandal of Charlie's mother's death,

I never dreamt that I'd have to announce to relations that he was a criminal with a fake passport.

He's exaggerating. He must be. We never fully tell the truth in this world. Even I know that.

A dread washes over me as I smell Faye's behind to assess if more poop has come out. He *is* Charlie Quinn. He has taken another identity because he wished to be someone else. Why? My stomach knots. I want to know more and I *really don't* want to know any more.

Charlie is totally entwined in the Ella O'Brien case. That is also clear. He stalls at times and looks to see if I'm going to accept him moving on. Why can't I ask him everything that I put on my lists in the evenings? Something always stops me. Like now, I should storm back in there and ask exactly why he's saying he's a criminal. Why has he got another name on his passport? Here I sit watching Faye play with the tassels on the bedspread.

I cannot imagine our Charlie being all that awful. I like him. He's right. I believe him and follow every stage of his story with empathy. I am being manipulated. Mother tells me I'm naive and gullible and perhaps I am.

The new en suite mirror shows me my shocked expression. I'm pale. I take a long hard look at myself. I cannot believe that Charlie would do anything as awful as Ella O'Brien. He would never harm his own child, he wouldn't...

Faye's babbling and comes in onto the tiled floor. I worry she will hurt herself all the time. She has no fear and stands there telling me her own little story.

I did wonder about Charlie taking her up the road on that first day here. He had wanted to escape, we could all understand that. I've used Faye as a means for that many a time.

There's an ache though. Was it just that he wanted company that wasn't judging him? It was just to have a presence that wasn't encouraging him to talk or asking him incessant questions. Of course, that was all it was.

Faye likes him. Children accept people. They've no fear, no knowledge of how evil people can be. I invited Charlie in, I encouraged his interest in Faye.

'Let him have her for another while,' I suggested to Joe when they were gone from the house for the walk the other day. 'It's good for him to be around children.'

I never dreamt that Charlie would have hurt her. When she came back she'd been crying inconsolably. Joe had found them both distressed and he couldn't explain why.

I'd been glad of the break. Glad that someone took Faye from under my feet as I tried to get the dinner ready for all those people. Others, like my mother and Joe, always allow Faye to come back to cling to me. I get afraid of Faye injuring herself with the hot water and the tiles in the kitchen. I'd been grateful of the time without her clutching my leg, or crying to be picked up.

'Go check on them if you like then,' I snapped at Joe, when he asked where they could be. 'He went to the left, down towards the sea. Go get them. Dinner is ready.'

'They can't have gone far!' Someone laughed. 'Neither of them are great on their feet.'

The sweat had poured down my back with anxiousness and the heat of cooking. I was sweltering until Faye returned in Joe's arms and Charlie tottered in looking as upset as Faye sounded. There was no explanation, of course, and he had cried almost continuously through dinner. Why?

'Jet lag, sad at being home, worrying about Ella. There's the dying thing too!' Joe suggested. 'There are plenty of reasons for why the old critter was upset. I wanted to join him in a sob or two.'

'What happened on the road?' I asked in a whisper.

'Nothing. I think they could only go that far as he was feeling ill. He got sick over the stile.'

I forgot the whole saga because there was no reason to think badly about it. Now there's a reason to think differently. A breath catches in my chest. There's worry in those mirrored eyes that I don't want to acknowledge.

If I tell Joe my suspicions, he'll be angry. Worse than angry. I'll be either making a mountain from a molehill or he will not respect my decisions anymore. It's taken me a long time to regain my own confidence about writing and if I admit that perhaps I've bitten off more than I can chew and have brought danger into our home – it'll be a disaster.

Standing in the bedroom, I look down at my notes. Charlie is seventy-eight by all of our calculations. He's terminally ill, can barely walk, and is weak as water – what am I fearful of? Charlie Quinn can do no harm to anyone anymore. My imagination as always is running riot.

'He's eccentric and will bring change into our lives,' I had insisted to Joe. 'It is a good plan to have him here for a while. Trust me.'

I gulp. Who can any of us trust? I know that I'm not trustworthy. Charlie believed in Ella and she let him down. He's obsessed with even the memory of her, and something has kept them apart for sixty years. Ella has never spoken of him. By all accounts she's not said a lot. Surely if she had a reliable witness she'd have brought him forward.

Charlie must've done something bad in the past that makes him a fugitive for all this time. I cannot bring myself to think an eighteen-year-old boy could do what is swimming about in my head.

He was a butcher; used to blood and death. A shiver runs through me. Someone like Ella should have clung to the likes of Charlie in her hour of need. Despite her court trial she never mentioned him. None of the newspaper reports mentioned Charlie. What hold has he over her? What makes him come here? My mind reels and thumps blood into my temples.

'He's a sweet man,' my mother said. 'Unusually quiet with a good heart. It's a pity he's missed all those years here with us all.'

She doesn't know that he has something to do with Ella O'Brien. Her face is before me and there's a telling-off in those eyes. She will explode.

'What have I done, Faye?' I ask. 'It's not safe for you to be here, my darlin'. What the hell do I do now? What the hell do I do?'

14

CHARLIE QUINN

Coming forward to say I was the father of Ella's baby wasn't possible. I reached the ship and was on the high seas before things really sank in. I'd no way of knowing what was happening back in Tyrone and as I chatted to a few other boys on board I became more concerned about my own dilemma.

'Indentured servant,' a boy younger than me said. 'We're white slaves. You'll have to sign a contract for at least three years to do work for some blaggard out there. How else do you pay for your passage, food and board in the great wilds of Canada?'

I learned too that being younger than I actually was might do no harm at all. Even though I wasn't one of them, for a time, I got lumped in with the British Barnardo's children. I soon got tired of that and instead became Charlie Quinn, a big fifteen-year-old Catholic boy from Sligo.

I knew of places and people in the county from extended family letters and could easily pass myself off as a Catholic. Being a Fenian made me like scum to the British boys, and I liked the southern Irish lads. I enjoyed listening to their way of speaking and I found myself mimicking their accents and cheekiness. I missed out on a childhood and while on board I had some fun and freedom.

The British didn't mix much with the Irish, which also suited my initial deception. The Irish all had a manner that was liked and I wanted to be liked.

People joked that I was big for my age. Being considered a child helped get me more grub and to the top of queues.

The only time that it proved a disadvantage was when I smelt whisky. There was no way they'd allow a child a dram, no matter how much you begged or pleaded. The alcohol took the pain away and I wanted to be lost in that nice haze. When I'd had my birthday with Jock I liked the sensations the drink gave.

It had drawn honesty from my heart and this was to cause the problems that had committed me to the course I was on. The demon drink would hurt me many times. It definitely started the chain of my tragic life.

I was trapped in a large tin cage many miles out on the Atlantic Ocean, with hundreds of other desperate souls. My family at home knew nothing about where I was or why I had disappeared. Anna and Cedric would worry. What was I to do? I hoped Jock might somehow explain my departure. Leaving these worries aside was necessary for I had no means to let them know – even if I wanted to.

In the bustle on board there were many who had no kin to care for them. For me, having no family to care about was a blessing. I needed to maintain the lie and be a child again. The truth was not a good idea and I stayed quiet. The majority made the best of the new adventure even though they were afraid. Looking out to the horizon we dreamt aloud of a country with new people and places to explore. We all had the chance to change our lives and names if we wished during these conversations. It was a liberation and an imprisonment at the same time.

Landing in St John, New Brunswick, I hadn't the time or the

chance to think much of Ella at all. The dread for myself was very real as we leaned out over the ship's side. We watched *The Lady Rose* of the Cunard Line dock and a heaviness entered my soul and it stayed there for many a long day. Running away from my crimes has never kept me free – if only I had known this at the time.

All of the fifty or more children travelling alone were handed a cardboard sign with a name and age. I made my own to blend in. Some boys swopped theirs about for fun. This meant in many cases we were not who or what our signs said.

This was not something I did. I was Charlie Quinn and had spent time and effort on my own sign. I wasn't going to give it away. Whether this was good or bad in terms of what was to come – I don't know.

We were all murmuring that we didn't like the look of the men and women sent to take us to what they were calling a 'receiving home'.

We all stood complicit and vulnerable. While we were waiting a balding, grimy man approached me and quietly said his name was Daly. Immediately, I clung to his sleeve and nodded that I was the young fellow he was after. Jock's relation had come to the rescue. I wasn't one of the 'homeboys' that the whispering amongst us was describing. Standing in line on the docks, I got the sense that the children with the signs were a class beneath the other people making their way to and fro. If we were glanced at, it was out of pity, fear or loathing.

I wonder many a time, what might have become of me if I didn't start my life in Canada on the back of lies. Would all of my life still have been the same if I was Charlie the man, rather than 'Charlie the homeboy'? Would my life have been easier as a free man with holes in his pockets? Possibly not – but we'll never know now.

Fran Daly with the balding head and greasy comb-over, took

me with him without saying much to anyone. Through his rotting teeth he muttered something about signing papers at the gate. He never did. I wandered after him, oblivious to what was ahead.

15

CHARLIE QUINN

F ran Daly spat a lot. He chewed tobacco and his loose shirt and trousers stank of something I couldn't place. I was to find out it was bad personal hygiene and the stench of cattle. The large Canadian cattle smell different when alive in the wilderness.

Leaving the docks, I remembered that I'd not said goodbye to the others. In my naivety I thought I'd see them again. Nothing in my simple brain had prepared me for the expanse of Canada. Ireland is small and most people know someone who knows someone else – or that's how it was. I was certain I'd see my new friends again. I never did.

'You're a fair big lad.' Daly spat out the window of his moving truck. It battered about the roads and I watched this new shining world I'd been waiting on. 'I've got a stable of workers and I think you'll make a fine foreman for them. Jock wrote about you and said that you've got butchering skills? The telegram said nothing much other than you were in a hurry to leave home.'

'Aye.'

I thought of asking this boney man for the papers I was to

sign but the dead animal in the back was smelling badly in the heat of the day. Something told me not to bother about how long I might get to work on his farm. I was in awe of the beauty of the countryside and he didn't talk much as he squinted at the road. His bad eyesight became a blessing later on in my time with him. With his bad driving on the dirt tracks I was afraid that I would never get to wherever we were going.

The homestead had big padlocks that held a high wire gate closed. It and the fencing were well-coiled with barbed wire. That should have told me all there was to know. Fran had things he needed to keep safe, or he had things he needed to keep from escaping. It was mostly the latter.

The one-storey homestead was wooden and had a long, new veranda circling it on all sides. The windows were large and covered in mesh and the door swung with a creaking sound as Fran's woman appeared out of it. When she was coming down the few steps I noticed her limp and lack of cleanliness. She was about forty maybe – or she looked the same age as Fran. She chewed tobacco as well. They might have used the same hair lacquer too as her tied-back hair shone just like his comb-over did.

'Selma,' Fran roared. 'This is the butcher boy from Jock's letters.'

With her hand to her head, she shielded herself from the sun, and me from the sight of her. I wouldn't see her often. When I did I shivered. I never forgot those times.

'I'll take him to see around,' Fran shouted and he seemed proud. I perked up, thinking I was a special visitor who he wanted to impress. My clothes were unsuitable for the climate. Daly's clothes weren't much better, and I shrugged off any notions of not fitting in.

It was the sunniest season and it was unbearably hot for an Irish boy. The sweat sat on my pale skin and the guilt dripped off me for stealing another ship-boy's clobber. I was glad of the small sack full of worn clothes on the high seas and foolishly I thought I'd get new Canadian ones.

How my heart sank when I saw the place Fran was showing off.

Two sheds covered in sods of earth were lined with filthy mattresses and heaps of rags. 'Home Boys' was the sign on the larger shed's door and 'Home Girls' on the other. He pointed to a foul-smelling drain near the far fence and said, 'Ditch for your filth.'

For miles as far as the horizon were crops and pasture. An odd, small head bobbed up between the potato drills and a horse or two could be spied if I strained against the light.

'Nobody calls here. If they do, there's to be no talking to them. You're all thieves and criminals and are treated as such.'

He really thought that of the other children. They were innocents who did nothing to deserve such nonsense. Saying that, Fran was right about me. As he spat and cursed about the demons of children he treated like dogs, I thought he was the worst of brutes. I was right, he was worse than I could have ever imagined.

I knew it was unfair of Fran to think badly of the children that needed to make this journey to a new life. Many of them were exceptionally well-reared. They were from poor homes and they were almost all biddable, moral souls. Even the boisterous boys kept themselves clean and were trustworthy. There was a need to please and survive in them all. Many of those cherubs were too young and fragile to travel alone. They were supposed to have chaperones. Most of these didn't do a very good job as there were far too many charges in their care. I had thought that terrible. Youngsters cried themselves to sleep and there was no help to tie the shoes they were given by the charity.

These vulnerable youngsters were now in places like Daly's.

I was old in comparison to them. When I saw the lines of battered shoes near the shed for the boys, I could tell that there were very small children about.

I should've run at that very moment – but where was I to go?

'I'll need a good right hand to keep this all in order,' Fran spat and gestured around the dusty yard. 'Selma doesn't like you lot mixing with our own. Don't come near the house. There's a few house girls who will take any important information indoors. If you can do what is necessary, I'll put you in charge of all the brats. Jock tells me that you'll be a good worker. He knows, of course, that we take in the rats off the streets from England and elsewhere and that we're in need of help to work them hard. He said you'd be a good pick for this position.'

The worry in me then was for the younger children I'd befriended on board. It was clear to me that day, standing in Fran Daly's homestead, that we were all doomed. Those same bright faces I knew from the ship would be in dumps just like Daly's. I couldn't bear to think on that then... or now.

He thumped my arm – like we were comrades. Vomit leapt into my mouth. I held it back and looked around. Hell itself might have been better. Charlie Quinn deserved it all and I knew that my sins had brought me to that place.

I cried.

Fran pretended not to notice and marched us across the yard to the fields, muttering instructions about the lay of the day; the rising times, working routines, the places for water, food, the rules, and the work that needed to be completed.

Did Jock Daly know how things were out in Canada? I doubt he knew it all. Like most people, he saw the migration of children to foreign places as a kindness. Listening to the dreams of most of the other boys on the journey, I knew they weren't expecting anything like this. I was shocked to the core. I was old enough with hairs on my chest and even I felt sick. How did a small child cope when their fate in the likes of Daly's sank in?

I can still see in my mind's eye the first small home-child I met there. She was a beautiful-looking girl of about eight years old. Her tattered dress was clean, and her blonde hair was tied in thin, white ribbons. She wandered out from around the homestead with a dog on a rope. It was a large, mongrel breed that was capable of biting large steers.

'She's one of the house girls. Simple Bridget we call her. Pretty little thing,' Fran said and I couldn't look at him. The tone was inappropriate for discussing a child. 'Isn't she lovely? And she's quiet, like you are. And one of my favourites. Catch my meaning, boy? She doesn't make trouble or cause me to lose my temper.'

'How long have I to stay here?' I asked.

I'll never forget the reply. 'Your sign said fifteen years old. That means three years. You're mine until you're eighteen. All of you savages are here until you work off your passage and your keep.'

'I'm that already! I'm almost nineteen! Jock must've told you that? He took me for a pint on my birthday,' I stammered. 'I was to be a labourer. They mistook me for a child on the boat. I let them think I was younger. I didn't want lumped in with the men. I'm sorry, I'm not fifteen. Jock will tell ya. I'm a man.'

'Trouble is starting from you already,' Fran said, standing back and with one swipe of his big arm he thumped me square across my jaw. I didn't fall over which surprised him. 'You'll need to work off the cost of your passage and lodgings. That'll take at least two years. We've other men here on the same ticket. Get comfortable and don't give us any problems. Ask the others what we do to the troublemakers.'

16

CHARLIE QUINN

Rhonda's tapes need changing and she's sniffing into a tissue. I've stopped watching her reactions to my tales. I don't want to dilute the message that is coming pouring out. If I look at her she tends to grimace or wince and that stops the deeply entrenched flow of the past.

For now, part of me still wants to seduce Rhonda into liking me. I also need to stop fading my failings into the background as the whole point of this is to atone for my sins.

'I must be truthful. I stole. I was a thief on the ship. I took a box of clothes that weren't mine. And food that should have been for more needy children. I did it just because I could. I used some of my thefts for good but mainly the crimes were for selfish reasons. Evilness crept into me, just like my father said it would.'

Rhonda wants to stop and wait until the tapes are ready. She holds her elegant hand out to stop the words and I do as she wishes. When she nods for us to resume, her eyes don't meet mine. She's disgusted, I can tell. That saddens me. Who can blame her? I disgust myself.

I didn't know that the climate was harsh in Canada. I'd no

idea of the cold. I'm sure my stealing meant some poor divil froze to death. I heard many children died from exposure and cruelty all over the country.

While trapped we all became ingrained with shameful gratitude. From the day we stood on the dockside with those cardboard signs around our necks, we all knew once they came off we would keep quiet about our origins.

The taking of his extra clothes and coat must have left him very vulnerable. Of that I am certain. Every child I saw needed the materials they came with to survive. I took the very thing he needed to live. Each letter of his name is stitched into the inner collar and I've kept that garment to this very day. In a few months' time, I would also steal his name.

'You don't know that he died as a homeboy?' Rhonda adds in and breaks me into the present. 'You're crying, Charlie. He might not have been lost to the cold.'

'I know I stole a means for his survival.'

'Didn't Fran Daly take any other children from the dock that day?'

'No. He had more than enough. Too many as it was. I know many other large homesteads used armies of children as contracted slaves. Jock Daly hadn't paid my fare there. Or at least that was what Fran said and I'd no means to ask Jock the truth. Jock had merely pledged me as a workman for years. It was normal. Some of the children were never paid. I did hear that some were lucky and fell into good homes and were well cared for and got schooling. The chances are, though, that Randal was treated worse than a dog.'

Rhonda makes us tea and a nice egg sandwich. I like boiled eggs, I always have done and I'm delighted as it travels with ease into my stomach. Rhonda has sent Faye to her grandmother's and I'm grateful for that too.

'Can I go on before little Faye comes home?' I ask when

we've eaten the majority of what's in front of us. 'The next part is hard to think about, never mind say out loud with a child in the house.'

Rhonda touches my sleeve and pats it. The touch is sympathetic but firm. 'I am glad to know that the name is from a coat. I thought it would be much worse. You are very hard on yourself. This is how it was in those days. Tough and bleak. You did what you had to. There's nothing you could have done to make the world better. Nothing any of us can do. We must try to survive and find happiness.'

I nod and gulp back the last of the tea in the mug. 'I didn't intentionally take his name. It will all become clear soon enough. I was Charlie Quinn on Daly's farm and at that time people thought that we would all have better lives in Canada.' I start to cry. 'Hundreds were sent and nobody knew or gave a damn about the likes of Daly and his ilk.'

'Oh, Charlie. Don't upset yourself. We can talk about all of this at another time.'

'I need to continue. Everything feels ready. I need this.' I dab at my eyes and lean into the soft chair and go back to Canada.

Within hours, maybe even minutes I'd made up my mind to escape Daly's. I'd left Ireland for something better and this was not it.

There were four labouring men and the rest were children. They were mostly young boys and the few girls were expected to work as hard as anyone else. My memory is not what it once was and I've wanted to forget my time there and my brain has obliged. Father's wrath was long since gone and Daly's fury surfaced that same fear all over again.

I was to bunk with the men in a byre and was told to lord it over the workforce of small hands and feet.

'There aren't many men here, or older children who are fit for this life?' I asked the menfolk and they didn't enlighten me as to why this was the way it was. There was little communication other than shouts and orders. It took me a few days of plotting and scheming to wrangle some information out of one of the older boys. He was known to be one of Daly's favourites.

'The mines. Those that cause trouble are sent to work there. When we start to cost money and effort, we are sent away. Don't bother to speak back or try to leave. You'll get sent to the mines if you try anything.'

'Has anyone escaped?'

'No point. They'll just take you back here or send you some-where worse. Everyone can tell who a home-child is. You don't need a sign around your neck.'

'We're the oldest. Why aren't there more boys our age here?'

'Once we get to be full workers, Daly's supposed to pay for that labour. Up until that he gets paid. It makes sense that he returns the older ones to the receiving homes. They're bad wee cunts by then anyhow. Younger ones cost him nothing and are only just landed off the boats. They're easier to tame. I've learned to toe the line. He's promised that I will work out my time here soon. I just need to keep my head down for a little while longer.'

I couldn't believe it. I was used to violence and still the badness that seeped out from around Fran Daly shocked me. The memories of there are all mired with the fierce threats and hard labour.

We weren't far from the coast and fresh river water. There was such beauty in the landscape and I let none of that register.

Daly saw that I was strong in body and mind. Jock probably told him that I had little conscience or morals. Perhaps he also wanted a companion, someone to condone or cement his methods – thankfully, I didn't fall totally for his indoctrination.

'You understand the ways of the world,' he said. 'A man with ambition can see why I'm hard on the youngsters. They need the work. We need the workers. You cannot be soft on them. God knows, though, we need better leaders to till the soil and reap good harvests.'

Daly was a mixture of a heathen and a religious nutcase. He ranted about the persecution of men with passion for the Lord while looking for reasons to hurt others weaker than himself. The experience of my own father made me wary of him. Fran was eerily convincing and the others seemed to fall for his methods.

If you pleased him, he gave you special treats, like some time off work and sugary snacks. I got these and I found myself wanting more of them. The grown men and all of the children wanted to impress the ugly bastard. He was our master. Having him smile at you made your sorry life easier.

The daily routine escapes my memory. The harshness of it shows itself on my hands to this day. I was allowed to work a mule and a horse sometimes. This was considered an honour as the animal did the hardest of the work. I hadn't any knowledge of farming or working animals and I lost my patience a lot. I'm ashamed to say that I lashed that mule brutally on more than one occasion.

The children were also beaten. I stood by and watched the other men help Daly. I worry that I beat them too and chose to forget it. I try to be honest with myself in the dark corners of my soul. I don't know if I took up a rod to whack a child. I think I'd remember such cruelty. I'm still not certain why the men hurt those youngsters. It might have been for sport or to relieve frustration; like I did on the mule.

I can still smell the sweat off Daly and hear the cries and also the silence after a lashing. I didn't partake in that brutality. I really don't think I did. I do know that Charlie Quinn shrugged it off and thanked God it wasn't his problem.

I also protected myself by refusing to make friends. Shutting myself off from the others was one way of not hurting myself or them. Randal Hamilton had been kind to me until I punched his nose in and stole the contents of his travelling trunk. I was afraid that I'd snap into the divil Daly and Father saw in me. Or worse still, that I'd be a victim myself if I let anyone close enough.

I was right to detach myself, because that little blonde girl I saw on my first day got too close to Charlie Quinn.

17

CHARLIE QUINN

Selma Daly, Fran's wife, never ventured far from the house. She tended the vegetable gardens to the back and sides with the home-girls. I only heard her hollering and screeching or saw her hobbling out to open the gate.

I watched their own children go off in the truck with their father. They didn't acknowledge or look at any of us. There were three of them. I paid as little heed to their faces as they did to mine.

I knew from travelling to the homestead that it was many miles from a main road and even more miles to find other people. I'd explored the farmland as much as possible and there wasn't another house within my sight line. The prairie beyond the cropland held their cattle and the talk was that it went on for a hundred and sixty acres.

At that time, my Irish brain couldn't comprehend these distances. I couldn't walk or run away in the heat we'd been having for the weeks I'd been there. I noticed, too, the times the family came and went. The gate was opened like clockwork in the morning and evening by one of the men or Selma. It rarely budged during the day. Deliveries were few and far between and if people arrived they stood and shouted to be let in.

To this day I wonder if the Dalys mistreated their own children. Possibly they did. At least the three of them escaped for a few hours every day. Although, it might be worse to smell a freedom and then have to return to the stench of imprisonment.

While watching them come and go, I figured that civilisation couldn't be as far away as I once thought and I made up my mind that once I got out that gate, I'd never return.

Daly was known to the authorities. Someone in a police uniform called quite regularly. I never saw his vehicle. Fran would become agitated and more aggressive before and after this man called. I hoped that he was a dutiful person who'd save us all from hell. Of course, for my time at least, the uniformed man never made any difference to the children who came in that gate.

Harvest time was tough work. Some of the children were not fit for the tasks they were given and I did double the work some days to cover their mistakes or inabilities. It was one of the loneliest times in my life and I prayed for change and escape – no matter what the price. I was taken at my word. Fate or God spat on my prayers.

Selma came out to meet me one evening when I was dragging the mule and the cart in from the field. Seeing her up close was shocking. She had a large scar that slashed the length of her face from a crumpled forehead right through her eye, nose, lips and cheek.

'I'm looking for Bridget,' she said and spat spittle at my feet. Fran and she spat a lot. 'Simple Bridget. You seen her?'

I knew very few of the others' names, as I didn't want to have them giving me more nightmares. Unfortunately, I knew little Bridget.

'Who?' I asked.

She didn't like my tone. I could tell by the turn-up of that mutilated nose. 'Little blonde Bridget. She walks around with the big dog. Simple, stupid Bridget.'

Everything in me curled up as I hoped Selma wouldn't find Bridget until she calmed down.

'I haven't seen her.'

I wanted to scream that I didn't know where Bridget was because if I did know I'd tell her. If it meant saving my own skin, I would sing like a lark about anyone's whereabouts.

Selma eyed me suspiciously. 'Jock's butcher boy?' she asked.

'Aye.'

'Fran about?'

'Out in the far pasture,' I lied. I wasn't sure where Fran was, I just felt that I had to know something or she'd knock me about for sure.

'You don't like us much, do you?' Selma grinned. A shiver took itself through to my bones. I was a grown man and I couldn't take being near her. 'Check the ditch. She might be out there.' Selma pointed towards the shit-trench.

Reluctantly, I abandoned the mule and walked behind the sheds with a hand over my mouth. There was Bridget. She was squatting, dress scrunched up, over the trench. I sighed with relief until I saw that she was sucking at a peach.

'Bridget!' Selma roared from her position in the yard. Bridget's shocked little eyes met mine and juice ran down her chin.

I placed a finger to my lips to tell her I'd be quiet and she should be too. With two more slow mouthfuls Bridget finished that peach and flung the stone into the muck. Quick as a flash, she swiped a sleeve across a wet mouth and fixed her dress.

Without a word, we walked back to Selma's figure standing with her hands on boney hips.

'Was she eating one of my peaches?' Selma asked. Bridget

kept on walking back towards the house seemingly indifferent to her theft or the question. 'Was she eating a peach, answer me.'

'She was taking a shit,' I replied. My tone was defiant. I was utterly stupid to try to be brave.

'Stand you there!' Selma ordered, pointing at me to stay put. Considering her bad leg, she turned quickly to grab Bridget by the arm and yanked her back towards the house. The heat of the day was leaving and with it went all my confidence. The squeak of the front door opening again told me of Selma's return. Brandishing a rifle in one hand and Bridget's blonde hair in the other, she hobbled down the steps dragging the child after her. She had that fierce gleam in her eyes – it's still before me now.

'Peach. Was she eating it?' came the question again and she let go of Bridget's hair. Cocking the rifle onto her shoulder she pointed it towards me. 'Answer! Or I'll shoot you like a dog.'

I couldn't look at those innocent blue eyes as I'd see the peach drool on the front of her dress. I closed my eyes. In those seconds I was sure Selma would gun me down. In a way I wanted her to do it.

I heard a scuffle of feet and sensed that Bridget had taken off running. When I peeked there was dust in Bridget's wake and the sight of little legs fleeing. I must have clenched my eyes shut again as it was another few seconds before I heard the shot. It rang out. Bridget staggered on for quite a bit, and as I fell to my knees, she slunk forward and ended up head first in the dirt. Her lifeless little body crumpled just a short distance from the start of the filth-ditch.

I scuttled over. The blood poured through her blonde hair and she flopped like a rag doll when I picked her up.

'That'll teach that husband of mine to give away my peaches,' Selma roared.

18

RHONA IRWIN

Joe drives in and parks at the front door as per usual. He'll slam the door closed behind him and dump all his stuff at the bottom of the stairs and make his way to the downstairs loo. He'll fart loud enough to be heard in the living room. It is the same every day and sure enough today is no different. Everything has come to a halt in my brain.

Charlie never bats an eyelid at the tension between his hosts. He ignores the life around him. Credit where it is due, it could be said that Charlie keeps himself to himself and is a good guest.

My trembling hand pours whisky and soda for us all.

'Upstairs,' I order at Joe through gritted teeth. 'Need to talk.'

I can tell from Joe's expression that he doesn't want any drama after accounting all day. He just wants to enjoy being home. I notice that he hasn't missed Faye's presence as he thumps up the stairs behind me.

'What is it now?' he says and sits on the bed. He has taken the crystal glass with him. Of course he has.

'In case you're wondering, your daughter is with my mother.'

Joe looks up. He is waiting on other news and knows that there is something more unusual coming.

. . .

I clench my jaw and fist. 'That man downstairs has a fake passport. He went to Canada when he was eighteen to end up as a slave and witnessed the murder of a young girl.'

Joe stops drinking to breathe in sharply. 'Murder?'

'It's awful.'

'He witnessed that as a young fellow? That would damage anyone. Lord. Murder? Charlie left one mess for another...'

'He's not sugar-coating anything and he's telling it all as it was; brutal, horrible things. He couldn't inform anyone of the murder as he was far from home and virtually imprisoned... There's a nagging doubt in my head because I've been doing some research at night and have asked my cousin, Margie, to look into things. She's a history buff. It's all a bit of a mess. I don't know how to explain it all.'

'I've had a hard day and what do you want me to do?'

Practical, pragmatic Joe sits on our bed looking tired.

'He's called a different name on his passport,' I say. 'Why have a fake identity if you're an innocent man? He's a criminal. He stole someone's name.'

'Many immigrants take new names and he only witnessed this murder. I take it that it wasn't him killing people?'

'No! He did nothing. It wasn't his doing. No.' I say that word slowly, picturing the scene on the Canadian ranch as Charlie described it just a short time ago. 'You've been trying to get Ella to see him. Has there been any word about that? Any luck? Why won't she see him? What does she know about that man downstairs? And why is she not talking about him in any of her revelations over all the years?'

'She hasn't defended herself very much at all. I think that's why there's been all of this interest. My contacts have only just heard from those dealing with her affairs. It's all slow. She's living in a convent. It's a closed order and they wouldn't pass on any messages. A PR company helped me and I doubt Ella even knows that Charlie is back.'

'Possibly not.'

'He's not said what he knows about her case then?'

I shake my head, jealous that Joe has a whisky to sip.

'He might have hurt their baby. He was a butcher...' I start.

Joe rises to his feet, incredulous.

'He took Faye off that day...' I start to explain.

'Stop that talk! That's ridiculous. Don't do this, Ronnie.'

'Don't do what, Joe?'

'Make everything worse.'

'Maybe he did more than witness bad things? Joe, look at me. It's easy for us all to believe that a mother might hurt her own and it's not easy for us to think that a man might?'

'Charlie's a good man. This is just typical! You were all about *his eccentricities* when he first arrived and about how wonderful he was. You were all on for him staying here with us. Now, you think he's some kind of monster? You were the very one who argued that Ella O'Brien should never have been let out of prison – it was you yourself that said she was beyond evil. Then there's a dying gentleman living here and he's speaking to you because he trusts you and you're doubting him. Why doesn't this surprise me? All men in your world are at fault in some way. We are all bad guys! Charlie, me, your father, everyone. What do you say to people about me when I cannot hear it?'

'This isn't about you at all.'

'For once I'm the good guy?' Joe spits in a low whisper. He turns his shoulder to shield himself and says, 'I cannot understand it. You look poor Charlie in the eye and pretend to like him – is that what you do to me?'

My mouth opens to tell Joe that I love and desperately need

him – nothing comes out. Joe gets off the bed and goes back downstairs.

As usual, I am the bitch.

19

CHARLIE QUINN

Rhonda pours another whisky and soda. I'm glad of it. There's been very little said over the dinner and the last few hours. We've checked on the news and with all the excitement of Ireland doing well in the World Cup, there's been no mention of Ella. I'm glad of that too. Things must be quietening. There's a foreboding. It is the calm before the storm.

Rhonda has told her husband, Joe, some of what we discussed. I can tell by his sympathetic expressions.

'We've had a hard day today,' she tells us all at the table. 'Thinking of the past is not all plain sailing.'

Perhaps she's justifying the whisky, her tiredness and my lack of speech to her husband.

'There's a lot more to go,' I tell them both. 'I think you're right, Rhonda – I should think about how I'll get to see Ella.'

Rhonda nods and sips her drink.

'Could I make arrangements to go to meet her? How do we find out?' I ask.

'Leave that to me,' her husband, Joe, says and I thank him as he takes his leave of us.

Rhonda, without asking, clicks on the tape recorder. I wipe

the sadness and potato from my chin and resume the painful unveiling of the truth.

I'd seen dead people before. Ireland's wakes and open coffins ensured I was accustomed to the sight of death but nothing prepared me for Bridget's lifeless corpse.

Selma screamed orders from her position in the yard. She didn't stray far from where she was. 'Leave her. Let them all see what happens to thieves.'

I placed Bridget back down gently beside the stench and saw the blood on my hands and shirt. Bridget's beauty was covered in dust and blood and I knew the others would be back from the fields at any moment. If they'd heard the shot they'd be running back by now. Selma wanted them to witness this before chuck-time and I couldn't leave Bridget like that for them all to see.

Selma continued to shout and the man in me rose up. I became determined and somehow got the strength to lift my rag doll. I walked towards the main gate. Where I was planning to go I don't know. Bridget weighed hardly anything at all, and even though I was petrified I walked on. I suppose that was brave. The guilt I carried with her was huge. I had failed to protect another child. That's all I felt – self-loathing and fear.

The gate was closed as usual and I waited as the dust was rising on the road. The truck with Fran and their own children was coming homewards. Selma stopped her shouting and never came towards the gate. I waited on a warning shot or even a bullet in my back. None came as I stood there crying.

That's where the past muddles on me again. Fran must have come home and taken Bridget. I remember clinging to the little body, and I felt the wrench of her being gone. There must have been discussions and tirades. That would have been normal for them and this was a mess. That is all gone in a haze of uncertainty. Did the Daly children see the murdered remains? Possibly. Did it affect them? I hope not.

Bridget's death killed another part of who I was.

'I should've saved her,' I cried at Fran as he made me unhitch the mule and see to my night-time chores. 'I should have taken that rifle from your bitch.'

Fran stood back a pace or two and gawped. That shook him for a second. He scratched his scalp and stared off into the distance. In his own weird way, he was upset too.

'Did you give her that peach?' I asked.

He nodded.

'Why? Didn't you know Selma wouldn't like it?'

'There was no harm in giving the angel a treat,' he said and sniffed. 'No harm in it at all.'

'There was plenty harm. Bridget died over a fucking peach.'

I'm not sure when Fran said what he wished me to do next. It cannot have been long after the incident. I can still see his rotten teeth and hear him say, 'We need to get rid of the body. With a bullet in her skull we cannot say she ran off or hurt herself. There's been too many things in the paper about deaths and runaways. This is all a real problem.'

There was a silence.

'Like... Selma could get into bother.'

He wanted me to do something. Nothing would have prepared me for what he said next.

He leaned closer to me and whispered, 'You'll have to bury her or maybe you could cut her up?'

This will never, ever leave me. Never.

I need to say quickly that I never laid another hand on Bridget. I would never have done what he wanted. Nothing would have made me do that.

Charlie Quinn, though, has stood silent until this very day about what the Dalys did. The only consolation is that I refused to do their butchering.

I knew it was only a matter of time before the other children started asking after Bridget, or about the sound of the shot. Fran and Selma would also want rid of the only witness who refused to dispose of the delicate little corpse.

I had to leave before they had time to think or make plans. When all was still, cold and dark I changed my clothes, took my sack of tattered belongings, put on the overcoat and crawled into the back of the truck under the stinking tarpaulin.

When I watched them leave in the mornings, the back of the truck was never checked. I prayed all night that this would not change. Trembling, I waited until daylight shone through the tiny hole near my nose. Listening to Selma's shouting, I started to shake uncontrollably and with each bang of the truck doors I wet myself a little. There, lying in my own piss, I heard the gate open.

My Ella's fate swung before me then. My darling might be hunched in hiding and fearing for her life. I prayed that she still loved me and Charlie Quinn was escaping again. He was leaving all responsibility for what was happening far behind him. Again.

20

CHARLIE QUINN

I shouldn't have left that day. I made many mistakes and the lack of options made it necessary for me to flee again. My bloodstained clothes were left behind. I was seen with the child's dead body. Then I was missing. I should have known that the Dalys would use all of this to their advantage. Charlie Quinn was a runaway, a murdering coward.

When the truck finally stopped, I heard Fran and the children get out and walk away. I slipped out into the street and felt freedom. I almost jumped for joy. Without taking in my surroundings, I kept my head low and mingled into the crowds of people along the wide, busy street. I didn't know the town or take stock of it. I was too afraid to believe I was fully free. I strode away as fast and as far as I could.

Talking to myself, I was convinced I was not a criminal. I was an eighteen-year-old and within my rights to leave Daly's. I had promised nothing about working anywhere for anyone and I was not a child. I had come to Canada as a man to do a man's paid work. Never mind the murder or abuse – I was a free person in the vast expanse of this new country.

In case I lost the run of myself, the smell of urine, sweat and the grime kept me grounded. I held on to the side of a tram and hoped I would not be noticed. I wasn't and the tracks took me along a few streets until the conductor shook his head at me. I dropped off at the next stop.

Still moving, I heard a steam engine's whistle. I instinctively sought out the train. Slipping past the guard was easy enough as the queues to the wooden platforms were heaving with people. They too were waiting on escape – or that's how it looked. I had no Canadian money and only had a few Irish coins left in my shoe. It was a cold day as I was wearing Randal's coat and the damp nature of my trousers gave a shameful chill. I didn't care where the train was going, I just knew that I needed to be on it. I watched the crowds and saw a lady struggling with her trunk. She had no help for whatever reason and she was looking perplexed.

She wasn't wealthy. I could tell that she was wearing her best attire even though it wasn't colourful or flamboyant. A wedding ring shone on her finger. I made my way down the platform and stood beside her, hoping she couldn't smell anything as I was upwind of her. That plain, middle-aged woman smiled as I tried to figure out how I might grab her purse in this mob of people.

'Might you help me with this when the train comes?' she asked, pointing at the leather trunk. 'It's very heavy and I need assistance.'

'Yes, missus.'

'Man of few words?'

'Man of no means. I don't have enough to even get on this train.' It had been a long time since I was an honest Charlie Quinn. My breath held and I looked up the track.

'Where are you headed?' she asked, not even flinching at my poverty.

I shrugged. She was taking in my appearance and possibly she got the smell then too.

'If you help me with the trunk, I'll buy you a ticket to Ottawa?'

'Is that far?'

'You are Irish?' she asked. 'Perhaps you should make your way to Manitoba. There's plenty of Irish everywhere and they are heading out to the prairies.'

'I'm not sure that I need more of the Irish.' My eyes filled with tears and I sniffed. She was shaken by that as she touched my dirty shoulder.

'Don't you worry. If people are honest and hard-working, Canada is a wonderful place. You'll find your feet and not look back from this day forward.'

She really believed it. The train was spotted when I was about to ask her where she was from. Everyone moved forward to get a good position for boarding.

The throngs got off and I didn't look upwards. I waited on the instructions of how to lug on the trunk with this stranger. She sat across the aisle and true to her word she bought me a ticket to Ottawa. I thanked her. It was generous because she was going only a short distance. I rose to help her get off again. She shook her head. 'No need. I've someone to help me now. Believe in the Lord and every blessing to you, Randal Hamilton.'

I hadn't told her my name. She must've read the label on the coat as it lay across my lap.

'Thank you, missus,' I muttered as she got off.

21

CHARLIE QUINN

I sat in Ottawa's station for a long while and was asked to move on a few times by the stewards. I couldn't leave. I was in shock. Extreme tiredness took over and ravenous hunger. With nowhere to go and no motivation to live, I was in grave danger of throwing myself under one of the trains. As night fell I held out my hand and sat on a low step with my head hung low. I wouldn't admit to begging. It felt more like praying.

'Get up out of there!' a man shouted and pulled me upwards before I had barely sat down. 'With arms like that you can shovel coal. There'll be none of that!'

Without much instruction I was set into the engine of a steam train and given a shovel. In no time at all, the state of my clothes and the stench was covered in coal dust. There was no need for small talk with the three others. The noise of the engine meant we had to shout and I had nothing to roar about. The rhythmic work was soothing.

The men left me be for thousands of miles. I hadn't much time to think or look around. The work was hot and hard, and appreciated. The breaks were short. I had a clean bunk with hot water to wash in when my long shift was over. I rinsed through some of my clothes and hung them in the moving air from the train to dry. I only lost a pair of good socks using that method. The food was basic, tasty and plentiful. The cool, clear water we got to drink reminded me of home.

'Money,' the chief stoker announced about three days into my train-journeying. I shrugged and this made him laugh. 'Make sure to get deals struck before you take on work again. I'm a fair man – many aren't.'

'I need a bed, food and a way to move. I would work for free. I like this work. Anything to help me settle into Canada would be fine. Thank you.'

'We can't keep calling you Irish. You are Irish, I take it?'

'Aye.'

'What's your name? You've no papers?'

'None.'

'We have to shout something at you when we need you.'

'Randal Hamilton. That's me.'

'Fine name. Randy, are you?'

'No!'

'We'll call you Hammy then.'

'Aye. That'll do.'

'Ham for short.'

'Grand.'

That was the way of life for that fortnight train ride all the way to the prairies of Manitoba. The lady on the platform had given me a name, a destination and target to reach. I wouldn't have known any place names until we were passing them on the train tracks. I'll be forever grateful to that nice stranger. Knowing one place and having one particular destination made it easy to focus.

Not talking had become a way of protecting myself from lying. I could also hide from telling the truth. The men asked very little about my life. They themselves didn't want me to pry into theirs. It suited us all to haul and shovel coal and stay quiet.

At some point on that journey, I got hold of a stack of recent newspapers. They might have been to clean my arse – I saw my real name in print. I ripped it out and kept it. I never found any other reports. This one was enough.

I open my wallet and hand the crumpled slip of old newspaper to Rhonda. She reads the entire article for us. Then reads it again without crying.

Murderer on the loose

Young Bridget Fahy is shot by Barnardo's Immigrant Charles Quinn

New Brunswick Sept 27th – Bridget Fahy (8 years) was fatally gunned down on the property of Mr Fran Daly, by immigrant boy Charles Quinn, yesterday evening. The bloodstained clothes and loaded rifle were left beside what remains of tiny Bridget Fahy. Following an extensive investigation and search, Quinn is still missing and considered deranged and dangerous. He is not registered with the nearest Barnardo's receiving home and the authorities have no record of him entering the country.

The name Charlie Quinn (aged 18 years from Tyrone) is on the manifesto for the ship, The Lady Rose, *from exactly a month ago. A considerable amount of cash is also missing from the Daly home. Quinn is described as 'a quiet menace'. Mr Daly and the authorities believe that Quinn was found out in a robbery by young Bridget Fahy and that Quinn shot her in the head before escaping.*

22

RHONDA IRWIN

Earlier, I watched Faye's breathing for a long time. She sleeps soundly and it's a joy to witness. I cannot take my mind to a time where children were herded like cattle, exported and left to the whims of others. As hard as motherhood is, how could I give Faye away? Or harm her? As bad as the blackness surrounding me has been, I cannot imagine not watching Faye breathe.

Joe didn't speak much since he came home. Functional communication is becoming the order of the day again. I've had a long phone call with Margie, my amateur genealogist. I played her some of the tapes.

'He sounds genuine,' she said. 'I believe him. They were different times, Rhonda. He was young and alone. I feel bad for him. What makes you worry? It sounds like you're making it even worse than it is.'

She was referring to my usual pessimistic outlook which family circles gossip about.

'I'll fax over some documents and photographs for your file,' she goes on. 'There was a Randal Hamilton and Charlie Quinn on the ship's manifesto. Also, Charlie's mother was found drowned in the quarry. The family folklore hid that one very well! It seems logical that Charlie was blamed for what happened on that Canadian farm. I'm finding similar accounts of indentured servants blamed for crimes and running away.'

'He says he's an expert at that. Running away, I mean. Then, I wonder why is he here now? Is he escaping something in Canada?'

'He's trying to put all of this right,' Margie replied. 'I can hear it in his voice. He's not running away anymore. He's doing his best, Rhonda. Give the poor man a break.'

Margie knows that I'm hard on everyone recently. The whole family knows that Joe takes the brunt of it all and I think that last statement was meant to hit home for Joe's sake as well as Charlie's. She confirms my suspicions when she asks, 'How is Joe through all of this? What does he think?'

'He's trying to get to Ella O'Brien. He wants to get permission for Charlie to meet her. Good old Joe has taken it on as his own private mission.'

'That is typical. He's a good-natured man.'

'Are you implying that I'm not a good person?'

Margie is silent on the other end of the line.

'Sorry,' I said. 'I didn't mean to snap like that. Sorry. Joe thinks I'm a bitch too.'

'Rhonda, we don't think that,' she says softly.

'I've been thinking a lot about Ella O'Brien,' I tell her. 'What must she have gone through? Whether she is guilty or innocent of the crimes, she must've been in such a bad place.'

'I'd say she is still in a terrible way.'

'There's been a lot on the television and in the newspapers. Everyone is speculating about it all. I pity her and I do feel for Charlie. I do. He's not being totally frank though. He's hiding something. I cannot put my finger on it.'

· · ·

I didn't want to admit that one liar can spot another.

'He's not finished though, Rhonda. He's got at least fifty years to explain to you. Of course, there's going to be more heartache. Are you sure you are up to hearing it all?'

I shouldn't have sighed loudly but it saved me from losing my temper. I waited a few seconds to compile an answer. 'I'm fine, Margie. Just because I've been to talk to a counsellor doesn't mean that I'm on the brink of losing my mind.'

'Of course not,' Margie said and I knew she thought me a little bit unhinged. They all do. Joe revealed to her that he'd dragged me to talk to someone after Faye's first birthday. I'll never forgive him for that. 'And Ella is no doubt very busy. All this publicity again will take its toll. And she's to be on for an exclusive interview on *The Late Late Show*! The whole country will be tuning in for that. Charlie will be nervous for her, I'm sure. Worried for himself, too, no doubt. She might finally mention him, especially if she finds out that he is back in Ireland?'

I gasped.

'Is he ready to reveal all to the nation, I wonder? Talking to you is one thing. Every paper in the country will be in a frenzy if they know he's the father of Ella's illegitimate baby. It won't look well for either of them. Maybe that's why Ella stayed quiet all these years?'

'I feel like I've opened a can of worms.'

'This is not your fault. We all know Ella's story is raked up every time there is anything even remotely similar in the news. Charlie coming home was his doing and you are lending a listening ear. You might not ever need to do anything with what you know.'

I couldn't believe what she just said.

'That's typical! That's what's landed us in this mess in the first place. Everyone stayed quiet about what they knew. You want to hush things up, pretend they never happened? Everyone is dishonest with their silence. I'm not like that!'

I'd been harsh and loud. Faye murmured in the next room.

'It seems that nothing I say is good enough. I'll keep sending on all the genealogy documents and things that I'm finding, Rhonda. I'll go,' Margie said. 'Goodnight now and get some rest. Ring me if you need anything else.'

I sit on the carpet next to the bed and sob a little into the towel. It's a relief and release to be alone and let out the anguish. I'm going to have to join the men downstairs and pretend that all is as it should be.

This was all supposed to help me better myself and my situation. It is making shit worse. Instead of dealing with anything, I curl into bed and pull the duvet high over my head. Where might Ella O'Brien be right now? I cry hard for her, for myself and for the children who have been cruelly used in the world.

23

CHARLIE QUINN

Ella has been in the newspapers again and mentioned on the television. In Ireland, everyone notices the national coverage. There is no escape.

The plans are for Ella to appear on the most-watched television programme chat show this Friday night. *The Late Late Show* is watched by the majority of the Irish population every week and there's a frenzy of interest brewing. We don't even put on the radio much during the day as Ella's section of the show is advertised a great deal and it stunts my thoughts and speech.

'What do you think Ella might say?' Rhonda asks me over breakfast. Faye's sucking the butter off long rectangles of toast. 'Should we tell RTÉ that you have some information to share?'

'I didn't come back to be on the television.'

Rhonda stops eating and looks at me intently. She's wondering what exactly I am here for. Still after the many hours of listening, she's not sure about the man staying in her spare bedroom.

'You're right. You might get into trouble for travelling on a fake passport,' she says. This makes me chuckle and gives an impatient gleam to her eyes. 'Randal Hamilton might come forward,' she says. 'You might hear about what happened to him. If we ask will we find him alive and well?'

'I am Randal Hamilton.'

Rhonda coughs and steadies herself before reminding me, 'You stole his coat, and his box of belongings on the ship to Canada. Isn't that what you said? And you thought that he had frozen to death in the bitter winters as a home-child?'

'Did I?'

'I can rewind the tapes and find it.'

I shake my head and hand. 'No need. I know where Randal is.'

'I've made enquiries, Charlie,' Rhonda admits. 'Each group of migrant children stood for photographs before they were sent across the sea to the receiving homes. Lists of names were taken. It was all very methodical up until that point in their journey. There was little follow-up of the children placed on Canadian farms. When I enquired they told me that a boy with the name Randal was in the photograph before departure from Southampton, and there's no record of where he was placed in Canada.'

'They didn't care where he went. I've been telling you that.'

'Explain to me, Charlie – where is Randal?'

'He wasn't the only child I stole from. I had nightmares about the others suffering because of what I stole. I've told you and Joe that I am a bad man. I've a great deal to explain and confess.'

'What has all of this to do with Ella O'Brien?'

'Once you know it all you will be able to help Ella. You will know what is the best thing to do.'

'Did you take on the name Randal to hide from the Canadian authorities? To hide from the murder of Bridget Fahy?'

I reach out to switch on the tape recorder she has under my nose all of the time. Sitting back in the chair, I return to the train, the clack of the rails and to my transformation into Hammy.

Fate, providence or luck had Charlie Quinn taken from me. From when the generous woman with the heavy trunk mistook me for Randal Hamilton, it seemed a good idea to be him. Then, after I read the newspaper clipping, it became necessary for Charlie to die along with Bridget.

I couldn't have changed the way things were, even if I did return. It was like when I left my Ella behind in Ireland – my word wasn't good enough. My version of events would be seen as lies. And Charlie Quinn, like the rest of us, tells lies.

Randal Hamilton could start afresh. He would be a good person, work hard and make his fortune. Hammy had a goal, an ambition and a place to reach. I was going to start life over again. There were many others doing the same. Even after disembarking the ship, children had swopped the cardboard signs around their necks to become someone else. This felt no different. Quiet, kind Hammy, with a wicked wit was born. I was pleased to meet him in the mirror every morning.

The engine hoots into Winnipeg, Manitoba, and Randal Hamilton steps off the train in a new set of clothes and an old coat.

24

CHARLIE QUINN

The National Transcontinental Railway united Canada and brought the ordinary immigrant into the heart of the country. It cut through forests, mountains and farmland. We knew the damage the surge of disease and people was doing to the native tribes. But no one cared. We were each out for ourselves.

I've learned a little about the culture of the Cree nation. Back then, we all just thought of them as savages and things to avoid. They weren't really *people,* you understand. They were like the animals – perhaps worse than that. Animals had value and the natives were more like vicious vermin. How I talked about and treated the Cree saddens me now. Over the years, I grew to respect and admire their ways. It will also turn out that I survived thanks to one of them.

In Winnipeg, I found a cheap hotel. The name of it escapes me. It was basic and clean, and had one of the prettiest serving girls I'd seen in a while. Polly Hollyridge was a beauty. As Ella was fair, Polly was dark-haired. Some Cree blood possibly coursed through the Hollyridge blood and I saw Polly as an exotic flower. She got some attention. The men were elderly compared to her teenage years and her father, who was the owner, kept his one watchful eye on his only daughter.

Mr Hollyridge was white and British (with literally only one good eye) and although I told him I was a Protestant from Tyrone, he saw me as a mucky, Irish Catholic. With him keeping Polly away from me, this made her even more enticing and again I had a goal to reach.

My Ella did come to mind when I was attempting a flirt with Polly. A young man has needs, though, and this creature was not a new love. It was lust. I suppose, too, she was a comforting conquest.

A few days into my stay, I took up the courage to ask Polly and her one-eyed father about work opportunities. I'd spent a great deal of time sleeping, eating, and practising my patter about who I was and where I was from. I'd made the mistake of mentioning Tyrone already, and when I said my name was Randal Hamilton, it didn't feel like a lie. It was a British-sounding name and I went with that. More flavour and colour was added to the story of where I was from and going to. Lord alone knows what spouted out and it took me all my time to remember the fanciful story.

Polly didn't smile a lot. I noticed that. There was little reason to be happy, and a smile was a rare commodity you didn't just use for politeness. They were for real emotion or friendship and weren't handed out to strangers. It became my daily chore to get Polly to smile twice. She wore her hair in a long plait and it reached to her arse. She wore floral dresses which covered those curves. I could make them out if I studied her well enough.

I helped out about the hotel and brushed the wooden walkway outside. I shovelled horse manure from the wide, dirt road into the barrows and lugged them out the back for fertiliser on the small drills for potatoes. Winnipeg was expanding and the compacted dirt roads could take some more of the new robust vehicles. Horses, though, were still the best form of transport.

I liked the atmosphere, it was less hurried, less flustered than Ottawa. There was a friendliness about Winnipeg too. The prohibition on alcohol was gone and I found out about an old speakeasy saloon up a maze of backstreets. Behind a small hardware storefront there was a larger saloon. It had a wild-west style I recognise now from the movies. It was an amazing place and old-fashioned for the time. A large mahogany bar with mirrors behind it welcomed you inside, a man with a moustache served bootlegged gin and whisky. Smoke and sawdust lay down below with sex up the three flights of creaking stairs. Someone on a bad-sounding piano banged on in the corner and drowned out the disputes and disagreements. It was a place of refuge for a drunkard. I came to know it better than most places in the town.

Manitoba state in the early 1930s was still a wilderness for wanderers. Despite the woman on the platform saying it was full of the Irish, it took me a while to find one.

I took it as a good omen when Polly's father introduced me to a fine man called Tom O'Brien. Instantly, I liked Tom's tall, sturdy gait. He wore a new felt hat and a tailored suit with pointed boots. His beard was clipped tight and it led into long sideburns that had a red tinge to their blond hairs. Tom's handshake could rattle your insides.

'Need a man good with cattle,' he said in a thick, Kerry accent. 'I've a ranch not far from here and we need a canny cattler.'

'I'm great with cattle,' I lied. I figured that I knew what to do with them when they were dead and that was a start. It wasn't the worst lie and I wanted to impress Polly. 'I'm a butcher by trade,' I added proudly.

Tom's eyes widened. 'Might use that sometime. Right now I need a cowboy. Are you any good on horseback?'

'I can run fast and I'm good on a bicycle,' I joked. There was no laughter. 'I'll learn fast,' I said. I hated to mention that my time with mules and horses up to this point was pretty bleak. 'I shovelled coal on the trains and spent time as a foreman on a homestead in Ottawa.'

'How long were you there?' Tom asked, rubbing his beard.

'Not long' – I nodded at the Hollyridges – 'I had the travelling bug until I reached here. I think that I'm ready to settle down and find me a wife and home.'

Tom smirked and reminded me of Jock. 'Family back in Ireland?' he asked.

'All dead. I'm an orphan and I'm not one of those Barnardo's boys or nothing. I'm nineteen years old, with a strong thirst for real man's work.'

'I can see something in you,' Tom said and thumped my back. 'How does $500 a year sound? $100 upfront, new shit-kickers and chaps, use of fine horse flesh and good grub?'

Polly put a hand on my shoulder and said, 'When does he start, Mr O'Brien?'

25

CHARLIE QUINN

Tom gave me a shopping list to purchase things under his credit at the local clothes and general store. Polly helped me pick out my new working clothes, boots, leathers and spurs. It was a good feeling to be getting new things all of my own. Hammy was a king for an hour. I also finally got to kiss Polly that day in the store when we were behind some shelves. It was nice enough but nothing like kissing my Ella.

Before I left Winnipeg I thought I better write to Cedric and Anna. As Cedric worked for one of the biggest newspapers in Northern Ireland, I thought he might be able to enlighten me about how Ella was doing. If tales of Bridget Fahy's murder had reached home shores he'd be able to tell me about that too.

I was still stinging from Jock's mistake at sending me to his cousin's but I needed to get a letter to my siblings. I wrote to Jock Daly and asked him to pass on other envelopes to Cedric and Anna. I didn't try to write to Ella. There was no way anyone would get a letter to her, even if I got up the courage to ask them to try to reach her.

I wanted to be many miles from where the letter was posted

in case anyone was inclined to find me. Hammy was cautious to protect his new life.

I went to the train station and asked my coal-stoker friends for help. I gave them a letter of thanks for the man who'd hired me in Ottawa and asked him to post my other letters home to Tyrone. Inside his envelope was a letter for Jock and inside it were two thin letters to Cedric and Anna. I explained to Jock that I had no return address other than the train station and my job as a stoker in Ottawa.

The stokers left, promising to bring back any return post that came for me to the train station in Ottawa. They were to leave it at the hotel with Polly. I didn't tell them I'd already got employment. I wanted to remain aloof. I trusted that they wouldn't read the letters and would do their best for a fellow stoker.

My stomach settled for the first time since I left home as I walked away from the station. It was a short-lived calm. That very afternoon, Tom O'Brien rode up to collect me from Polly's. He had another horse tied to his own.

'All set?' he asked and pulled the biggest, meanest, blackest horse from behind him. 'Here's yours. Let's get going.'

Polly stood with her usual expressionless face and watched. I was mortified. I'd seen the men expertly jump up on the finest horses in the past few days and there was no way I'd practised this as diligently as my lies.

'Umm...'

'Polly will give you a leg up,' Tom scoffed and it took me far too many attempts and embarrassing fails to get the beast to stand still until I got my leg over it. Polly laughed openly and this made me mad. I left without even saying goodbye as the horse took off at a canter and I had no confidence to slow it down.

My arse hurt by the time we reached the O'Brien ranch. It

was seven long hard miles from the outskirts of Winnipeg. Although similar to Daly's farm it had no locked gate, just a high gatepost spanning the width of the track. On it was a sign: *Welcome. Kelly Ranch.* It was well-painted and nailed securely on the wooden post. About half a mile down the track from the sign was the homestead itself. It was an impressive, two-storey wooden structure with a long, pretty veranda. Large shutters hung on the tall windows. There was money about the place, I could tell that straight away. The outhouses were a good distance from the main house and the stables and smells even further away still. The largest and tallest daisies I ever saw were clumped and swaying in the breeze all the way around the house.

'Were you ever even on a horse before?' O'Brien snapped when he took my reins. 'I've never seen a more uncomfortable bollix on the back of any animal.' He started to laugh too hard at me rubbing my backside. 'You'll have a sore hole for a couple of days until you get the hang of it.'

Tom was always correct.

The bunkhouse for the ranch-hands was near the stables. It was clean as a whistle. Rows of single beds with blankets and clean sheets that all smelled fresh. There was an odd hammock hanging from the big beams. An order, purpose and pride shone out of the place. Tom liked showing me around and I compared him to Fran and the ranch to Daly's.

'You have an eye for that Polly?' Tom asked. 'She said that you'll get married once you make enough money. How much is she after?'

My expression must have been one of total shock, cos that's what I felt.

'You have bigger notions than Polly then?' Tom teased. 'Thank fuck I've no daughters to worry about. You're far too pretty to be a bachelor. I better warn you, too, that the bossman,

Gus, will not take kindly to the look of you on a horse. He's expecting a good pair of hands for this job.'

Tom was right to warn me of Polly's intentions and about the attitude of Gus Kelly. For as much as I immediately liked Tom O'Brien, I hated Gus on sight.

26

CHARLIE QUINN

Gus Kelly doesn't deserve much of our time, but unfortunately, he is pivotal to the course of my life. Short in stature, with a balding, thirty-year-old head, he didn't look anything like Tom. In time I learned he was a stepson and that made better sense. The other men loathed Gus Kelly almost as much as I did. Gus paid the bills and our wages and we all bowed and scraped to him.

He was a bitter bastard, and called himself 'a real Irish patriot'. I wasn't sure what that meant and considering he never set foot in Ireland, I thought him the biggest ass going. Somehow, he'd heard that I was northern Protestant and this jarred with his pretend Irish patriotism. He thought that I was a chancer. He could see that I was not a good cow-poker or horse rider – therefore my fate with him was sealed from the get-go.

'Randal Hamilton,' he spat and got off his horse. 'I'd batter you, only we need men.'

I remember he ordered me out into the wilds of the prairie in the dead of my first snow and harsh winter. I was to roam the perimeter fence which was possibly six hundred miles give or take. This became one of my main jobs. At the time, he was sending me to my death. I knew nothing of the wilds of the prairies, in the snow.

Tom wasn't keen on the prospect. 'He'll die on his first night. Let's send the Chief with him?'

Chief was a Cree and I doubt he was called by his right name either. Silent and proud like I wished to be, Chief didn't complain. His skill for those first days out in the wilds of winter kept us both alive. He showed me everything with no need for much language. I learned quickly – or else I'd have died. I'll never forgive Gus for that time. Never!

The weather got that bad even Chief wouldn't venture any further. We made our way homewards at the peak of the storms. Thankfully, Gus took Chief's word that the fence was fine as far as the border to the west and that even he wouldn't move in the new, deep snowdrifts. I'd seen no fence at all, but I said nothing. This kept Gus happy until the days became more like a Canadian spring.

During the days with less activity, I used a rope, learned how to ride a bit better and practised rustling. Between that and the survival guide from Chief, I felt more able-bodied. Tom also had me butchering. This brought back old memories and skills, and even Gus couldn't mock my abilities at that.

It was when I was allowed into the main house for a Christmas meal, that I saw Gus's wife, Olga up close. There were very few females and even though she wasn't as pretty as Polly or as stunning as my Ella, she was shapely, brown-haired, and the men all called her 'cosy'. They also said that Gus purchased her from nomadic Russian workers. Before I'd been to Daly's I might not have believed that there was such a lawlessness to life in the wilds. Olga smiled and seemed happy in the big house, and when I caught her eye I knew she was as lonesome as I was.

I'm not sure how Olga and I came to be in the corridor together. No doubt I made excuses to be alone with her. When I brushed past I touched her sleeve. I expected Olga to shout out when I pulled her closer. She didn't even whimper. My mouth met hers and she moaned. I was shocked and stumbled us against the wall. I kissed her good and proper until we thought someone was coming.

I liked it. I kept thinking that I had stolen something from Gus Kelly. It was childish – that's how I was. When I got back to the dining room, my smirk was hard to quench.

Everyone still called Tom O'Brien's wife, Mrs Kelly. She was a grey-haired woman who looked much older than Tom. The Canadian prairie life sucked the youth from some women. Their beauty always fared worse in the prairies.

Mrs Kelly was intent on watching me. The house was very fine, with proper expensive furnishings and drapes. I wanted similar when I made enough and I started calculating how long it might take me to come by the means to impress people like the Kellys' wealth did.

'You're a fine young fellow,' Mrs Kelly said towards me more than once. She was tipsy and all of the scene enraged Gus. He sat giving me dirty looks and feeling up Olga, his wife. I could only smile and raise my glass at the distinguished, drunk Mrs Kelly. Tom winked, unconcerned about his own honour, which was understandable as his wife was, of course, out of bounds.

The cold store where we hung the carcases was where I met Olga again. It became our place for elicit rendezvous. It wasn't lovemaking. It wasn't anything special. Olga liked to think it was something greater than it was. Every time I got inside her I revelled in it silently for days. Smugly, I stood with folded arms as Gus Kelly ranted and raved about the work he needed done. I think at some point I must have boasted to the others. Possibly after some whisky, or over food in the chuck-shed, or while dreaming in the bunkhouse. We rarely went to town and I never wanted the seedy whores. So, they might have believed me and remembered it for the years to come.

If I did venture into Winnipeg, I usually went to see Polly. There was little made in the way of promises. Somehow she seemed convinced that we were engaged. This was awkward as I appreciated her finding me the job. I thought she was attractive and she didn't care that there was little of substance or love between us. She clung to my arm whenever I went to visit and asked about my savings.

Her father didn't think much of Hammy. I respected him for that. I agreed with him on most things. I thought he was right to protect Polly and I told him that.

'I've not asked Polly to get married and I never will.'

'She's promised to someone else, you know. If you don't want her, stop coming back here,' Mr Hollyridge said. That was the last thing he said. I left a little bit sad and rejected, and of course, I said nothing to Polly. The man was right.

It was just before my first big trip out to do a round-up, that I was told to come to the big house kitchen. When I opened the outer screen door, there was Polly standing with the other women.

Olga's eyes were brimming with tears and Mrs Kelly was angry as her tone was clipped as she said, 'Her father is dying. She's looking to speak with you. Says you're engaged.'

'The hotel?' I asked. I knew the place was a good earner and although the work was hard it wasn't cold and damp, or hot and sweaty. 'What will your father think?'

'She was to agree to marry her father's choice or she'll lose the lot.'

'I'll keep my promise to you,' Polly said, those dark eyes expectant and full of love.

I was a bastard as right there in a stranger's kitchen, I

rejected her. 'There's no engagement. We've made no such promises.'

'That doesn't matter,' Polly protested and made a fool of herself. 'I can't marry that old man. I've come to be with you.'

I didn't know who the man she was promised to was until I had to go and ask if there was any post for me. He was possibly ten years older than Polly and not exactly elderly or awful-looking. I was surprised when Polly chose to stay in Mrs Kelly's for she gave up her home and birthright for nothing at all.

I think Tom's wife, who I called *Old* Mrs Kelly, was relieved to have another woman about the place. If she knew about me fucking Olga she possibly thought having Polly there would stop all that. Old Mrs Kelly was generous and gave Polly and I a small, new cabin to the right of the main gate. We were to be a lookout beacon and when I was away on the range, Polly could stay in the big house if she wanted to. We never made vows to each other or were churched in any way. We lived as man and wife when I came back for a few days every few months. Then, I was off again.

I found life under the stars or under a canvas tent preferable to being controlled by Polly. She liked me to be clean and talkative. These were two things I was becoming less and less interested in being. When home, lying with Polly became boring and Olga took whatever energy I had left.

Neither of these women were my Ella and I was soon to learn what was happening back in Ireland.

27

CHARLIE QUINN

Polly took to staying in the cabin even when I was away. I was away for months at a time. I hope now that she had love in my absence. If not, it was years of her life she lived alone.

I was territorial and proud of my harem of two women. Other men were alone or with whores and I revelled in having two all to myself. And both of them doted on me. I couldn't brag about this and this bugged the show-off in me.

Hammy was becoming a wealthy enough cattle-hand and I was starting to think of home more and more. I was delighted when I went into Winnipeg for there were a few letters to me, in what was Polly's hotel.

'Fine place you have here,' I said to the man behind the desk. It was the man Polly was to marry who now owned the place and Old Mrs Kelly told me that he was a far-out relation of Polly's. There was no mention of Polly between him and I. Like I said, he seemed decent enough.

I took the bundle of envelopes tied in a small string. Cedric and Jock had taken me at my word in the letters and put c/o Randal Hamilton on the front.

It took me many days to pick up the courage to open the

letters. I was lying with my bedroll propped under my head watching the cattle drink from one of the brooks, when I finally ripped the paper open.

I read Jock's first and it didn't say much. He rambled on, telling me that his own wife had passed away shortly after I left. This didn't bother me none as I never thought much of her. Jock admitted that he was lonely as hell without us both. There was a mention of a few customers and it was very pointed that he didn't refer to my Ella at all. Jock was about the only person who knew some of our relationship and he failed me with a very short and unhelpful letter.

Anna's epistle was a lengthy novel. It read just the way she talked; full of her hopes for a good marriage to the new apprentice in Daly's butchers and of all the stupid books she had read. Anna mentioned looking after Father more, which I skipped over. None of her news interested me in the slightest and she didn't seem to miss her wayward brother one little bit. I shouldn't have expected as much. I hadn't spent a lot of time in her orbit. I was angry, though, and ripped her words up into tiny pieces.

Cedric's letters were last. There were two from him. I was thrilled and devoured every word. I wish I still had them. I read them over and over. The words stung and went something like,

And that Ella O'Brien, she's been the talk of the country. Taken away for murdering her own babies. Poor Dr O'Brien is beside himself with grief. Losing her and their good name all in one fell swoop. The poor man is distraught and who could blame him? She's going to be tried soon. Talk is they will be lenient as she's from such a good home, there's not much real evidence and this heinous crime is more common than we ever knew.

His words were painful, as he, of course, had no true love for

Ella. He also denied all lustful feelings for her too. I'm sure all men did at that time. Everyone considered her to be a wicked woman. I was disappointed that Cedric didn't enclose a paper clipping. He did mention:

I doubt you want all the sordid details. Working in the paper I get to hear all the awful news and I hate taking it home with me. I knew you'd be interested in Ella O'Brien though. You had such a soft spot for her. Aren't you sorry now you ever laid eyes on her? The whole place is mortified to be associated with her.

I am tired of all the horrible sins in this world. Someday soon I would love to feature a good news story. Send me nice tales of Canada. I will get a good journalist to do a feature on you when you make your fortune. I only work in the print setting. I was glad to read in your letter that you got work on the railway. What adventures you've been having. Write again soon and we can tell Father about how you are making a great life for yourself in a whole new place.

Cedric didn't go on about his own life, as Anna did. The second letter was a bit more revealing about Ella. I also cried when reading it.

Ella O'Brien has been in the papers again. Such is the interest in her, the stories run and run with no new details. We know very little about what happened that night. She's been before a special court sitting and you'll not believe it, the country doesn't believe it, she's been given a reprieve on her sentence. She's allowed to walk free as she's promised to stay in the care of some order of nuns! Can you credit that? If she were a man she'd be hanged! It's a disgrace. Something tells me that I should want to help her. As a sinner she's in need of guidance from a higher power.

I held the rein of my horse tightly and screamed into the loneliness. Whatever had befallen Ella was signed and sealed by now. Charlie Quinn was wandering free and was not held to any creed. Looking out onto the prairies I vowed to try to take Ella there someday. I felt her close even though she was thousands of miles away behind damp stone walls and locked doors.

Right then and there, I started talking to her soul. I promised us both, 'The truth won't be quiet forever, Ella.'

The cattle moved at their own pace and I followed. Mostly, I was alone and that was the way I liked it. Sometimes Chief came along too and we went on ahead of the herd and checked on the fences, the watering places or sometimes we left them with other workers and came back home. It all depended on the seasons, the weather and the workload back at the ranch. It also depended on what excuses I could find to be away from Polly. Gus mostly let us be.

I got much better at tending the herd and showed willing to brand cattle flesh. If I do say so myself, I was good at the work and I thrived on the terrain.

I wanted to tell everyone back home just how successful Charlie Quinn was becoming. All I felt was fear and guilt when I read Cedric's letters. I had lied to him about who Randal Hamilton was. I said he was a benevolent employer. There was no mention of my involvement with Ella or in the death of Bridget Fahy. Cedric also didn't know of the real connection between Randal and myself. Jock, too, mustn't have had any idea of what happened on his cousin's farm. He accepted me moving on to work on the railway and showed no sign of knowing that Fran and Selma wanted me arrested. There was no word in any of the letters about the murderer, Charlie Quinn.

Thoughts angered, though, when I dreamt of my Ella. She

was imprisoned in a convent and as I looked around at the wide expanse of freedom I owned, with the thoughts of two sexual partners on my return to the comforts of home, I cried for Ella.

What type of existence could she have in a cold, austere convent? I couldn't think of a place less suitable to her personality and beauty. I'm sure she was grateful for the reprieve, joyous at being away from the doctor and his family. I doubted, too, that a married woman had taken on the habit of a bride of Christ. The numbers for the holy orders weren't falling in those days and Ella would have been just another sacrificial woman to the power of the church. Her family would possibly have paid for her keep if she wasn't ordained. Her relations would have been glad about the lack of prison time. There was no shame of execution. This would have been considered a blessing to her people. What might Ella think of it though?

I aim to ask her that soon. Did she enter the order willingly or was it a terrible compromise she shouldn't have had to make in the first place?

28

RHONDA IRWIN

Joe's bare feet pad over the tiles and he comes to find me at our kitchen table. I should tell him everything. Start at the beginning with our lives, as well as with Charlie's. Would Joe forgive me my lies, like Charlie forgives his Ella? I doubt it. His hair is fuzzed up like it does when he's been sleeping. He rubs at his eyes and peers into the gloom.

'Can't you sleep?' he whispers, looking up the dark corridor towards Charlie's room. Coming closer to me at the table he turns over a few pages to skim their contents. There's a folder and a list in front of me and I wonder for a spilt second if I should try to explain my muddled mind.

'My brain keeps whirring.'

'And you went to sleep with Faye again. Didn't we talk about that? You need to get your body back into a normal rhythm. It's not healthy for either of you. You're now wide awake in the middle of the night.'

'I was shattered. It's a long day here alone with a baby and Charlie's story is making me very emotional.'

'I'm sure it is.' Joe sounds empathetic despite the time on the kitchen clock reading half-past three in the morning. 'He must be nearly finished with it though?'

'No. Not really. I just feel like there are more and more questions for him to answer. The deeper I go into this, the worse it gets.'

'Like everything in life.' Joe smiles and reaches for a glass in the cupboard. The sink's tap makes a gurgling noise as water flows into the spout. 'He was telling me a little of it while you were upstairs. He really loves Ella O'Brien, even after all this time,' Joe says incredulously.

'Some people's love lasts.'

Joe clumps the glass downwards. It makes a crack as it hits the worktop surface. 'That's it!' he whispers. 'You're jealous. That's what it is. You're mad as hell that Charlie loves Ella despite all she did. You think that I don't love you anymore and you're jealous of her.'

His face blurs as my tears come.

'Am I right?' he asks. 'Are you going to admit it?'

'Do you love me? Do you?' I ask, wiping away a drop that has trickled to my trembling chin.

'Rhonda, for feck sake,' Joe hisses.

'Do you love me? It's not a trick question. Even after the hell I've put you through since Faye was born – do you still love me?'

Joe pulls a hand through his hair. He stares and whispers, 'I've never stopped loving you. When are ya going to believe that?'

I don't answer as I rub the back of a hand across my cheek to remove a tear.

'You don't fully believe what Charlie tells you either. And you're jealous of his love for Ella. Pull yourself together, Ronnie. People have been through much worse and they don't sit in the dark mooching about their bad lives.'

'That's right.' I choke out the words. 'That's right, Rhonda is always the ridiculous one, the one who's going barmy. Rhonda is the one who doesn't believe people, she's the one who has problems that are stupid. I'm the burden that everyone thinks has a screw loose.'

'Here we go with the drama again. You always have to make things worse. You make simple sentences turn into an argument. Stop turning and twisting everything.'

'I love you,' I tell his back as he grips the sink. 'You don't seem to worry about my feelings for you. You don't need reassurance like I do.' Tears choke me slightly and flow freely now. 'Yes, I'm jealous of Charlie's love for *that* Ella O'Brien. Does that make you happy? I'm jealous as hell. And he's considered a great man despite all the wrongs he's done. He thinks he can just waltz back into everyone's lives and be accepted. No matter what he's done – he'll be forgiven. As he's talking I empathise with his plight and feel his anguish. At the end of the day I'm angry with myself for allowing him to manipulate me into liking him. That makes me angry too. I know that wouldn't happen for me. I'm not even forgiven a few bad days. I'm not forgiven for losing myself for a few months and for being uncertain about things. I've done nothing criminal, and still I am the one begging for love and forgiveness.'

'Why can't you just give in to liking the old sod and listen to his story without all of this anxiety?' Joe asks, turning towards me. 'What would be awful about simply loving, listening and believing someone?' He grips my arms and lifts me into those strong arms. He smells like our bed; warm, safe and secure. 'I love you, Rhonda. Stop with the hysterics and let's go back to bed.'

The kiss is the first passionate one we've had in months. I don't want it to end.

29

CHARLIE QUINN

Rhonda has a notepad and a list of questions. She sucks on the tip of her pen thinking of how she's going to broach the subject of having queries now about my ramblings. I don't have time or interest in her concerns. Friday is fast approaching and Ella will be on national TV baring the truth to the nation. I need to have offloaded most of it by then.

'I'm sure you have questions,' I start. 'I'm conscious that our time is running short. I still have a way to go before getting to the point of all of this.'

Rhonda sighs.

'All will become clear,' I promise, as if she's a child waiting on ice cream.

'We know that Ella was taken in by the Sisters of Good Hope. That much has found its way to the tabloids. I doubt she became an actual nun?' Rhonda says. 'She won't have been allowed to take vows after all she did? Women like her might be in the laundries or offices.'

'Regardless, she'll not have had any quality of life.'

'Does she deserve one, Charlie?'

'Do I? Did I?'

Rhonda doesn't know what to say as she breathes heavily and looks out into her garden. 'Having Faye makes me think of what she did,' Rhonda says. 'I cannot dwell on it.'

'Ireland was a different country then,' I say, sniffing back the sadness she brought between us. 'Ella might have been a totally different woman in today's world.'

'I cannot see how.' Rhonda's lips tighten together. She's like the rest, consumed with hate, despite the drought of facts.

'Ella is brave to come forward now and I am proud that she will try to speak out. I aim to help her.'

'We will all find it hard to understand how you can still stick up for her and love her, unless you know what actually happened?' Rhonda asks. 'When might we get you to see her, I wonder?'

'I worry that she will refuse to see me.'

'If she does, I'm sure that will be hurtful.'

'I deserve all that is coming. I hope that she gets some understanding and peace for raking over all of this.'

'Is talking helping you, Charlie?' Rhonda asks.

'It's strange hearing that name again. I like it. I've missed it.'

'Despite your illness and all, you were right to come home and be heard as well. That young, unnamed girl who gave birth alone in the old bathing boxes near her home has started all this Ella interest again. The poor little baby almost died and the girl is being questioned. Every time there's a case like this, Ella gets mentioned. It's as if she's never going to be forgotten.'

I nod and hold my protruding gut which is hurting me particularly badly since she started this conversation. The lack of control about where Rhonda might take all of this bothers me. I know where we will end up and I want to get there my way. As always, I need to be in charge.

'I'm wondering about a lot of things,' Rhonda says. 'I'm thinking of Randal. For some reason I want to know about him.

He stays in my mind. It's just that you stood into the Barnardo's boys' photograph too after *The Lady Rose* docked in St John's, New Brunswick. We've got it blown up larger and the small blurred head is definitely you. Randal Hamilton is the name for your position in the photo. How is that?'

'I told you I stole his things and then took his name.'

'Where was Randal?'

'I'd broken his nose and he was told to stand out as he was bandaged up and I stood in his place.'

'Oh I see.'

'You're convinced he's important?'

'Yes.'

'Don't worry about him now,' I say, getting crosser.

'Did you write many letters home? Why did Cedric think you'd passed away?'

'I never wrote home again. I disappeared from life into the wild Canadian prairies. Neither Polly nor Olga knew my real name or my past. If more letters came to the hotel I never collected them. I felt bad for a long time that I selfishly didn't write again. Considering what was following me, I felt it for the best. I didn't want Cedric to know the trouble I'd got myself into.'

'Have you left family behind in Canada now who might be worried? I asked you that when you arrived, you didn't answer me. Do you want to call them and let them know how you are?'

'Charlie Quinn has always been a loner.' This makes me sad again and I start that old-man crying I've been doing. It forces Rhonda into putting the kettle on and tossing her notepad away.

'Click on that recording device like a good woman,' I urge her, when I can catch a breath. I sip a soothing sup of very sweet, strong tea. 'If you're all ears I'll tell you about what happened next.'

30

CHARLIE QUINN

I was only about twenty-five years old when all hell broke loose at Kelly's ranch. I should have known that it was only a matter of time before Polly found out about Olga. I was a young buck with no sense of loyalty left in him.

I think Olga is like me in personality. She wanted to boast about her extra-marital partnering and she couldn't tell a soul. Olga also resented Polly's independence in the cabin. Polly had time alone with no in-laws looming over her, more importantly Polly had time alone with me.

There had been a few family Christmases in the big house with no issue and for years life was going all my own way. I had become complacent and uncaring about their feelings.

It was a Christmas Eve when Polly was visited by the boss's wife. Olga was feeling barren and stifled and she laid out the truth to Polly good and proper. Poor Polly was distraught.

I don't recall the many conversations I endured afterwards. I was cruel and told Polly that she'd have to make do with the situation. Polly thought she might be pregnant at that time, and the mistress's husband was both my enemy and overseer. There was no way Polly could make a scene about any of what she knew. We also weren't married and she'd left a perfectly good business and prospects to be stuck with me, therefore she had little choice in the matter.

I was brutish and unkind. I was a trapped animal and all I knew was to either run or fight. Don't they call it fight or flight? And at that point, I couldn't flee as the snow was many feet deep, we were expected at Old Mrs Kelly's table, and I thought I had a baby on the way. I wasn't going to leave another woman holding the problem I helped create. Polly was relieved to hear me say that I would be responsible and look after her and the possible baby. I also made it clear that the affair would have to continue as we'd have lost everything otherwise. I explained that I would try to escape from the liaisons in the new year but I couldn't promise how Olga would react. We were in a pickle.

Things continued on exactly as before. Each woman was unable to speak or cause a fuss for fear of what would happen to their own situations. The tension of being found out was a turn-on for the hot-blooded boyo, Charlie Quinn.

In the middle of all of this following chaos, Polly miscarried. I've always wondered if Polly lied to me about some or all of this. Who could blame her, I suppose?

I walked a tightrope of women's emotions and it was only a matter of time before I would fall. In the middle of that mess I felt grief for my child with Ella. I didn't acknowledge that at the time, and there was a lot of me hidden. With that and the disappointments – I was drained and unstable.

Alcohol started to be a bedfellow of mine when the women and the past were all too much. The whisky heated me during the cold spells and cooled my annoyance during the humid summers. Where it loosened tongues for some men, I made sure from then on that it did the opposite to me. It tightened my lips and resolve.

I also started to hit Polly when the walls closed me in and I couldn't get to be with Olga. It was wrong to hurt such a lovely woman.

Charlie Quinn wanted it all. He wanted freedom, and a family. One good woman was not enough for Charlie *Bloody* Quinn – he wanted two. He wished to be alone and in the wide-open spaces. There was nowhere he was happy and even at the bottom of a bottle he found no solace.

On the trail or being out with the herd meant I would dry out from the drink. There were only so many bottles I could fit on a chuckwagon along with the other supplies. In ways this was helpful. Once back with Polly though, I'd overindulge in the whisky and resentment.

It was after one of the longest trips away that I came home and slept for days from booze and tiredness. It was Polly's screams which woke me. I had my hands about her throat. Struggling to her feet, she managed to fend me off and made for the big house.

It was Gus and Olga who came to Polly's aid. They didn't tell Tom about the ordeal. They arrived into the cabin and took care of everything. I hated that Gus had the upper hand and he saw me upset. He was in charge when I was weak and I was angry at his kindness towards my Polly.

Again, the darkness descends on the bad times in my life and I remember snippets of those terrible days with Polly. It was easier to take off again, so I did. This time when I left for months, Olga and Polly came to some sort of arrangement or understanding in my absence. When I came back that time, Olga supported Polly. She called and took us food and invited Polly away into town in the truck.

I got jealous. They weren't supposed to console, or find solace in each other. I preferred when they just loved me. I was excluded. In a stupid way, I felt betrayed by them both. I knew it was me who was the untrustworthy partner and yet I was playing the victim.

Whatever happened between the women, Polly left Kelly's. I was drinking worse than ever before. It was maybe the next day I heard them both packing Polly's things. I was no doubt drunk. I should have gotten up and stopped her. Although, I couldn't have begged for Polly to stay in front of Olga. I was very conflicted. I wanted Polly to leave more than I needed her to stay.

I think I knew Polly should go too before I did something terrible. I had never truly wanted Polly or her pregnancy. They weren't part of the plan I had for my future.

The mess of it was my fault and still I did nothing to make things better. Sadness filled me, though, when whisky didn't and for a long while the drinking was all I cared about. Me and whisky.

My belly burned on as I muttered to an imagined Ella and I promised her the sun, moon and the stars. It was easy to swear oaths to people who couldn't hear them.

31

CHARLIE QUINN

Rhonda gets off the couch to make some lunch and doesn't turn off the recorder. Does she expect me to do it? I think about asking her. She seems angry now, thumping the items out of the fridge and sighing heavily.

'I told you I was a bad man.'

'You just were horrible to those poor women. You never told me what they said in their own words. Not once. It's as if they are not important. You used those women and abused them too! I cannot stay quiet about your behaviour in this session, Charlie. I just cannot nod and smile and pretend this is okay.'

'Polly left. I believe she went back to the hotel. Olga told me that she married the man her father wanted and they lived happily there. I believed that and was glad of it. She was safe. There is a happy ending.'

'I will find Polly,' Rhonda announces. 'What was the name of the hotel? She might still be living. Cedric might have written more letters to you and she might have them to this very day. Normal people don't destroy letters. Polly might have kept them.'

She aims to hurt my feelings with her tone. I've never been

normal or followed the rules of life, therefore her insult doesn't hit its mark.

'I never saw Polly again and I got no other letters from home.'

'We will look into the name of that hotel and making contact with Polly.'

'I don't see why *we* should.'

'And Olga Kelly, is it? What became of her? Why is the farm named Kelly and Tom O'Brien was the main man?'

'Tom O'Brien was married to Old Mrs Kelly. I suppose she wanted the Kelly name kept on the land.'

'And Olga? Where is she?'

'All will be become clear in time.'

'You just rattle off years of your life and expect me to accept it with no questions, with no interest in the women you've hurt.'

'I should've known that you would take the woman's side to this. I'm disappointed, Rhonda. I saw you as an objective ear. I told you I was not all sweetness and light. Why are you hostile now? I've told you worse things, surely?'

She busies herself with making scrambled eggs.

'What part of this is bothering you the most? Does Joe beat you?' I ask her. 'Is that it? Something about this story has hit a nerve?'

This silences the whisking and she takes time to think before she whispers, 'Of course Joe doesn't beat me.'

'He's had an affair then? Didn't he want Faye?'

Rhonda doesn't answer. I can hear Faye's cries from the next room and it changes everything. Rhonda disappears in a flurry of annoyance to get her. When they return Rhonda is very subdued and Faye is all ready for playing. The noise of the battering of dollies off the floor is very distracting. We start to eat the meal Rhonda has made without talking.

'There is something you want to say,' I mumble between

mouthfuls. 'I know you are helping me since I got here and you've been more than good. I can tell that there has been something bothering you now.'

She eats and passes bits of bread to Faye who smiles and babbles to herself.

'A problem shared is a problem halved,' I say. 'You're listening to me and it's making you angry.' I stop and wait for her to deny that. She doesn't. 'You're unhappy at the way I treated Polly and Olga...'

'I...' she says, taking a deep breath. 'It's not that as such. It upsets me to see things that worry me in your past. That's all. There's something I'm ashamed of in the back of my mind all the time and I'm not sure I should say any more.'

'Joe is bad to you,' I say, knowing he's too soft to be a brute.

'Of course he isn't.'

'You're about to cry. Tell me what's wrong.'

'I've no right to judge anyone. No right to think that I'm better than you.'

'No,' I say.

'You felt trapped. You ran or didn't want to stay,' she says with a stammer and pauses. 'I can see why and I worry that Joe feels the same way.'

'Joe is a good man.'

'I still worry.'

'About what exactly?' I ask.

'I had Faye to keep Joe with me,' Rhonda admits suddenly. 'I don't want it mentioned again.'

'I see.'

'Once I am cleared up here you will have to go on with this story. It is Thursday and tomorrow evening is Ella's interview.'

'Joe said he'd find a way to get me to see her.'

'And he is a man of his word.'

I notice that Rhonda wears no wedding ring. How I missed it before is beyond me.

'And he cares and provides for his family,' I say. 'I can see why you wanted him as a father for your child. I'm sure he's glad to be with you both?'

Rhonda closes her eyes and holds back some tears. It always amazes me how we take other people's pain back to our own. This has nothing to do with Rhonda, and now I feel I should be consoling her. It does grate on the old nerves. I resume my seat on the couch after taking the noisiest toys away from toddler fists. Faye ignores me, which is interesting. She, too, has had enough of me.

Settling into the soft fabric, the recorder still plays and I return to my cabin on the Kellys' farm in Manitoba.

Tom O'Brien was not a man to shirk responsibility therefore he wasn't one to hand over the reins of the business either. He was known as Mrs Kelly's man. This didn't bother him. Tom was sure enough of himself to deal with that. Gus and him were at loggerheads most days about some management issue. Like I avoided Father back home, I started avoiding the disputes between them. Olga was stand-offish following Polly's departure and I stayed away from her as she might have said anything in the heat of some big family dispute.

It mustn't have bothered me all that much, because I still took off on the usual drives and stayed away for months. A year passed without much incident. I was without a woman's company, and the bottle did me. The world was in turmoil, too, with talk of another world war. With it came the rise of more reasons for men to sacrifice themselves. Nothing could have seemed further away from the prairies and I was grateful for the grasses, the wild flowers and the sight of cattle roaming free. There were fun times playing tricks on each other and horsing about like children.

The round-up of the herds happened twice a year and these were the most tense times on any ranch. All hands were called on for the roping, branding and sorting. Tempers were high and patience was low. Gus was never good with leadership. He got very riled at the men and even though I was now a good hand on a horse and an excellent cow-poker and butcher, his wrath centred on trying to make me look foolish.

We'd come to blows many times. Neither of us had won the fight. Both came out of the frenzied fist-throwing after a few minutes, with unnecessary cuts, bruises and bloodied noses. It was not a surprise to see us tussling in the dirt. The other men just walked over or passed the two idiots punching each other.

My popularity was not high on the ranch either. The men resented that I still had a cabin to myself, when some of them were longer employed. I think there was awareness of me laying with the boss's wife. They didn't like that I had knocked Polly about a bit either. Polly had been kind to the men who got measles, tuberculosis, or ailments. She'd nursed them back to health.

I found it hard to make true friends, and although I'd have drinks or jokes with the men, I preferred time away on my own. For a young fellow under thirty, this was odd. For an Irishman it was even more than unusual. People don't like those unlike themselves. I had held on to my Irish accent and way of speaking and this also seemed a bone of contention. They wished for Hammy to either be a jovial, Irish buck or assimilate quickly and become a Canadian cowboy.

Gus Kelly and I were possibly bunched together as two pains-in-the-butt. The men put up with us, because we were both favourites of Tom's and everyone respected Tom O'Brien.

Tom was ageing well and showed no signs of slowing down in his work or thoughts. He could ride a horse better than any man I've ever known and he was fair and broad-minded.

Nothing seemed to rise his anger and other large ranch owners travelled many miles to ask him for advice or to buy his stock face to face. He was considered a man of standing and a decent boss. I was lucky that he had a soft spot for me – the underdog.

Charlie Quinn had plans and ambitions. He wasn't going to be the odd, orphan Irish boy forever.

32

RHONDA IRWIN

When I told Charlie my secret it was shocking how relieved I felt.

Three years ago I stopped taking the pill. I stayed quiet about it. There was no lie or trickery. Joe was reluctant to commit and I was nearing thirty. He never asked about birth control and he never blamed me when it had apparently failed. I didn't consider it as a lie until it was me who felt trapped. Then, I floundered about what I had done to us both, and to Faye.

'Rhonda makes plans and in fairness she does stick to them,' Mother says often. 'She has ambitions, lord love her, that's why she gets depressed. Like, she needed published and that happened. It wasn't a great success and then she wanted to have a family by the time she was thirty. And, well, Joe didn't propose. Is that it, dear?'

Thankfully, Mother hadn't started this conversation at the dinner for Charlie. Joe always asks her to stop putting me down and she listens to him. The usual plethora of sentences are said by the time she is silenced. The quietness around things can be worse than what is said.

'Women nowadays want it all,' she'll add. 'In my day, you

learned to be content with your lot. You waited and worked hard to find a man. Then if a healthy baby and a lovely home came you were grateful – what more do you young women want?'

'Thank Christ my mother is long gone,' Joe will reply. 'She'd tell you that women should achieve greatness and shouldn't give up on it just because they have children.'

'She was a hippy before her time.'

We all ignore that Joe's mother committed suicide. Even Joe's father does. He'll sit alone at family gatherings and smile in all the right places.

'I suppose you learned to accept things when Rhonda's father left?' Joe asked when Mother started the tirades of my failings just after Faye was born. There had been an explosion of anger. It had been weeks before she spoke to anyone in the family. We all knew not to mention this again. At the time, I resented Joe for provoking her. Looking back, her absence had given me some headspace when Faye was tiny and it also hid the home truths she pokes out.

'I'll never leave you,' Joe promises regularly. Still my heart throbs with guilt. 'Stop trying to make everything wonderful, Rhonda. It is what it is. Much as I hate to quote your mother, "we must learn to be content".'

Listening to Charlie these last few days, I wonder did I trap Joe and I. Was his reluctance to commit because he still loved another woman? Is he waiting on someone else to come along? I want to be the one true person who would totally fulfil him. I need Joe to marry me. Desperately. Ireland in the 1990s is still not ready for us to be living in sin. I cannot understand how Joe just won't commit. If only we could get past this.

Charlie talks of loving Ella yet he settled down to decades with others. Look what happened to that way of doing things. There are parallels to be drawn between the past and the present and it's hard to fathom what to make of all of our lives.

My cousin, Margie, has given me more information. She dropped papers and photographs through the letterbox, without ringing to say she was passing. I hadn't heard her at the door either. I've been argumentative and she slinked away before there was more of the same. I'm becoming more like my mother every day and that sticks in the gut too.

'Charlie is somehow connected to Ella O'Brien,' I warned Mother on the phone earlier. 'He's not told me everything and that's why he's home.'

'Huh! Rubbish. He came home to see what money was left to him. Like all those foreigners, he came back to see what he could get his hands on.'

That was all that was said on the subject and I moved on to meeting Faye's new childminder and how well it went. There was no point in lingering on the truth. Like the rest of us, she will learn soon enough what Ella O'Brien has to say.

33

CHARLIE QUINN

It took me a bit of time to win Olga back into my arms. I spent many a cold hour waiting for her in the meat store. I was still butchering, and doing it well. I got more and more work packing the meat from our best animals for the homestead, surrounding neighbours, and places in the town. Olga started supplying them to fill her days and to use the new truck Tom bought for the ranch. With my arms bloodied and the stink of death around us, Olga and I kissed for the first time in a long while.

'There's something sinister about you, Hammy,' Olga said. 'I know I shouldn't go near you, and that makes me want to all the more.'

She liked the movies. She watched any film she could find. I was one of those unsuitable men women always fell for. I didn't try to be, mind you. In those days, I never watched such nonsense.

Olga, though, relished those clicking reels of film. Being a plain woman in the wilds, surrounded with filth and men, I suppose it was only natural for her to escape into the glamour on the screen.

'You're married. I seem to like married women,' I pointed out that day after years of ignoring this fact myself. 'Are you with any others like this?'

She flung back her palm and slapped me square across the face. It stung and the knife on the counter looked interesting for a few seconds.

'Of course not!' she squealed and crunched her bosom against me. It was all very cinematic. I see that now. At the time I thought her a little deranged. She knew what I did to Polly and she provoked me by slapping me first.

'None of us like Gus,' she whispered in my ear, as if it were a secret. 'He bought me from my family as I was one of the first English-speaking, hardy Russian women to come to these parts. He doesn't want me working and making improvements. Tom stands up for us and I know Gus is as mad as hell about me driving the truck and making money. He's not giving me a son, and that's my fault too!'

I didn't want to point out that I had failed in that respect as well.

'I wish we could live in your cabin together. Let me leave him?'

I flung her away. 'Are you stupid? I make good money and am paid by your husband. Do you think we'll just move into the cabin together and I'll stay in my job?'

Years before, Tom's wife, Old Mrs Kelly, died in one of the worst measles outbreaks. Gus and Olga waited for the respected Tom O'Brien to find a suitable woman to replace Gus's mother. The Kelly name on the gate was in jeopardy. Tom was no blood to the land itself and Gus spat this at him on more than one occasion in arguments.

With all of this in the background, when I saw Gus fall from the hay loft it was easy enough to let him die. I did not get him any help.

Rhonda gasps, like Gus did.

The metal plough broke his fall and possibly his back. He twitched about a bit, like a dying animal and turned to face upwards. Running for assistance was futile and there was no way in hell I felt bad about Gus Kelly's death.

The mourning was fake. Few cared why or how he fell. If they did it was put down to a terrible twist of fate. Tom clung to me at the graveside. He gave me the biggest hug I ever got from a man and said, 'I'll need you now more than ever, Hammy. More than ever, my boy.'

I'm smiling now as much as I did that day. I was Tom O'Brien's boy. The fires of hell were a long way off. That hug was more than money or land. I was no one's boy, since my own mother died.

As Tom needed a son, the drinking subsided. I was also taken in to eat an odd meal in the big house with Olga and Tom. We would discuss the plans ahead. I always play a long game. Tom liked that I wasn't rash and impatient like Gus used to be.

'Now Gus's mother was a true pioneer,' Tom told Olga and I. 'Mrs Kelly staked her claim out here as a woman and started her homestead alone, with one rusty rifle and a mangy dog. She could shoot anything from a galloping horse. It was unusual for women to be allowed to own land, and she wore breeches.' He enjoyed the tale. I could tell by the gleam around him that he admired and revered her more than lusted after her. 'I was like you, Hammy. Young and good-looking then, with strong arms and an energy where it mattered. She was spoiled before I met her. Taken against her will by some brute. Gus was a toddler and she needed a husband. Things were changing and it was neces-sary for her to make a business arrangement with a man like me.'

Tom waited until Olga was in the kitchen to add, 'If Olga had a child with Gus, I would have been left with nothing. Everything was down on paper. You need your own papers now, son. You need to get working on your future.'

There was no need for Tom to tell me this as I'd thought of little else. One of the reasons I wished to be sober was to have a clear working head for the next steps in my plans. Getting proper documentation was going to be difficult and this bothered the ambitions I harboured.

Fate or fortune started to smile on Hammy when it was turning its back on millions of others across the globe. As part of the British Commonwealth, Canada was, of course, a willing ally for the Second World War. Although there was no immediate pressure on me to show interest in enlisting in the Canadian military, I heard that other undocumented immigrants were accepted and were easily written up on official documents.

This suited Randal Hamilton – who had no intention of ever going to war.

34

CHARLIE QUINN

The recorder gets clicked off. I reluctantly return to the present, I don't want to have to deal with the repercussions of what I have just revealed. There's more to come and I'd rather put up with it all in one fell swoop.

'Gus died?' Rhonda spits under her breath. 'You just casually drop that into the conversation and move on?'

'You did say we were in a hurry.'

'Don't be cheeky now, Charlie! Gus was your boss and your lover's husband, don't you feel anything about his death?'

'You didn't even know the man.'

'He was still a person. A human being.'

'Thousands – no, millions died in the months and years that followed, and those poor bastards died too. What was I to do about them all?'

She doesn't know how to answer me for a while. 'War is different.'

'Is it? What's the difference?'

Rhonda goes pale.

'Each one of us is capable of the most unspeakable things, my dear Rhonda. Don't you know that? Just because you're here in this nice home, with a perfect baby and good food, doesn't mean you won't lie, cheat, steal or even murder to survive and thrive. Haven't you lied and cheated too?' I ask, ignoring the raging headache and throb in my side.

Hands go over her ears and I wait.

'I found newspaper articles from your journey out to Canada,' Rhonda says softly. 'I've been doing some digging and not a great deal of sleeping. A relation called Margie is an amateur genealogist and she's been helping me do some research,' Rhonda goes on.

'Oh yes?'

'She has found the Hollyridge Hotel. It has been renamed and Margie found it.'

'Polly's place. How great.'

'She's trying to trace where she might be now.'

'Can she do that? I'd love to know about Polly.'

'Would you?' Rhonda asks, peering at me. 'Would you like to know about some of the others in your life history? I doubt it! I've been playing back the tapes and I'm sad about all you've been through, Charlie. But still I cannot pretend to be unaffected by it. I cannot condone some of your behaviour.'

'You're all annoyed about Gus? He fell from a height onto a plough. There wasn't much to it.'

'The genealogist is looking for the real Randal Hamilton as we speak.'

'Do you know I can still see his face if I concentrate hard enough,' I admit. 'Little, meek Randal with the very large coat his mother gave him. It was to last him for the years he'd be apart from her. Would you believe I still have that coat and it's in my case? Lucky for you, I had it professionally cleaned as it did pong from years of wear. Randal's family must've been wealthy at some point, as his clothes were of good quality. Like many others once hard times hit, there was nothing for it. You had to abandon your children or send them away. Imagine if Joe regretted lying with you and you had no option and had to give Faye up? Harsh times, Rhonda. Yes, Randal Hamilton was presented to me at just the right time and him with his much-too-large coat.'

'She'll find Randal, no doubt. I'm almost afraid to ring her with more of this information. It's getting more and more awful. I know you don't want Joe to know much... but he's asking me things.'

'Does he know your secret?' I ask her.

The pale jaw sinks with her shoulders. 'What?' She breathes out quickly with the word.

'Is Joe organising for me to see Ella?' I ask, changing the subject.

'Were you threatening me? I won't help him with that anymore,' she says. 'I'm taking Faye to my mother's until after the weekend.'

'I understand. When does your friend call? Is it once I'm in bed? I'd say that conversation is interesting?'

'I'm taking Faye and I'll be a few hours.'

'Off with you then, my dear. I'll ask you to set the tapes. I want to continue in your absence.'

She stalls in her departure. Does she want to enable more of my mutterings? I say no more and hobble to get a glass of water. From the sink I hear her change the tapes with angry clicks.

35

RHONDA IRWIN

Gripping the steering wheel, I try to lower my shoulders and relax a little. Tears spring up and Faye babbles in the back seat about, 'Driving to Granny.'

'Yes, Mummy is escaping to Granny's. That's a new thing for Mummy to do,' I admit. 'When I get there I should ring Daddy and tell him all about all of this.'

'Daddy,' Faye says and laughs. Despite her mother and grandmother, Faye is a relaxed, calm child.

'Mummy doesn't always tell the truth and it is a bad thing,' I tell Faye, peeking at her in the rear-view mirror.

'Bad,' Faye echoes. 'Bad, bad Daddy.'

'No. Mammy is bad,' I tell her. The word Daddy is much more fun to play with. She starts a song of her own making about her precious Daddy.

'Can I ask you to look after Faye again?' I question before we were even in Mother's kitchen. 'It's just this Charlie business. Faye is being neglected.'

I have presented Mother with an opening to criticise my parenting and it is ignored. She stands back as I hand over Faye's overnight bag. 'I doubt that she's abandoned,' she says, squinting at us both. 'Is everything all right?' she asks, peering closer still.

'Yes,' I lie as usual. 'I've just left Charlie talking into my tape recorder and Faye's expected to play by herself and she's getting no attention. Can you give her something nice for her dinner too, please?'

'I always do,' Mother replies, still studying me carefully while wiping at her shining worktop. 'If anyone wanted to listen to my life, it would make a good book. Ach sure, there's no interest in little old me. Is all this work you're doing with Charlie going to be worthwhile?'

'I don't know.'

'When does he leave?'

'Soon.'

'I've said to Joe that this may not be good for you. He reassured me that it was helping you write again.'

'When did you talk with Joe?'

'I dunno. Couple of days ago. I rang him.'

'At work?' I know how Joe hates being interrupted at work. If she's annoying him there, he'll be extra cross and I cannot blame him if he is.

'It was just before he was going home,' she says. I know she's lying.

'Don't annoy him. One of us nagging at him is enough.'

I've left another gap for attack. She ignores it and hands Faye an ice lolly from her freezer.

'And are you writing?' she asks, clicking on the latest electric kettle that cost as much as a cooker. 'At least you're getting dressed these days, that is an improvement.'

'Pardon?' I say, sitting on the nearest chair.

'With Charlie in the house, you have to look someway decent. That will help your relationship. Not that I know what makes a man stay.' She grimaces. 'I'm sorry that your father left us, Rhonda. I've never said that to you before. I am sorry. I was young and foolish to think I might change him and you missed out on things. I've been thinking that maybe all that with your own father is making you worry about Joe? That maybe your father leaving has affected you more than I want to admit?'

Her dyed hair is tilted, waiting on a reply.

'Joe is fine. We're fine.'

Faye's lolly lands on the floor and she scoops it up and sucks on it some more.

'What is going on then?'

'Ella O'Brien is going to be on the *Late Late*,' I say. 'You'll get a shock if she mentions our Charlie Quinn.'

'Why would she do that?'

'He fathered her last baby.'

'He never!'

'Apparently so. He was only eighteen and then he ran off to Canada.'

'The poor man.'

Her reaction to another man shirking his responsibilities is still the same.

'He's not totally innocent.'

'He didn't make her do what she did?'

'There's a lot more to the story that I cannot explain now.'

'I'm sure.'

'It's on my mind and even when I'm not listening to Charlie, I'm looking through the things Margie sends me.'

'She said she'd uncovered a lot for you.'

'Did she tell you anything else?'

'Like what?'

'I've been snappy recently, especially with her. I've had a lot on my mind.'

'She never said that.'

'Good.'

'And how is Joe?'

I look at the clock on the wall with the big hands. Joe will be almost finished at work and I should call him.

'Charlie doesn't want to answer any of my questions. It is very frustrating.'

'Is that your way of saying that yes you are taking all of this out on poor Joe?'

'We're having a hard time. Once Charlie goes, things might be better.'

'I cannot see what Charlie has to do with you and Joe?'

'There may be a scandal when Ella does this interview. What will you make of that?'

A slender hand touches my sleeve. 'You and Faye are my world. Nothing else matters. You need to stop waiting for things to be better and make the good times happen now – before it's too late. Go home and sort things out with Joe, that's the most important thing.'

I nod, fearful that my mother is right.

36

CHARLIE QUINN

Tom wasn't best pleased at me talking about joining a foreign fight. When I mentioned that I'd get my name in black and white on government documents he saw the need for him to vouch for me with the authorities. Having a man like Tom say you worked closely with him for the guts of ten years was a hundred times better than any piece of paper.

In June 1940, Randal Hamilton, a Tyrone-born, Irish Protestant was registered for home service in the war effort, at the ripe old age of twenty-eight.

Tom also had a word with some high-ranking uniforms. They needed meat and Kelly's was branching out with investments into meat-packing and production. With my knowledge of butchery, we were doing well, and a military contract was going to be very lucrative. Tom made great deals with the war raging across the ocean. This meant that Hammy was a needed, valued man right where he was in Manitoba.

'I need to fight,' I explained a few times to Olga and Tom over dinner. 'I'm no coward.' The drinking glasses glinted as I licked gravy off the china plates between speeches. I was a fervent fighter when safe in the big Kelly homestead. 'As much

as Gus was an Irish patriot, my own people were British. I need
to go with the others to war when the time comes.'

'You're going nowhere,' Tom said. 'You're staying here.'

That was all I needed to hear.

Olga had invited me back into her bed around this time. I
like to think she saw grit and bravery in my performances. The
sex was functional and it made me think even more of my Ella
and the whisky bottle. Staying in the warm luxury of a nice
house was something that kept me grounded and focused. Tom
turned a blind eye to my sneaking out the back door before
breakfast, and he didn't put a stop to the progress I was making.

It was rare that Canadian women who owned property were
allowed to run it by themselves. Whatever way the wills and
legacies worked, Tom and Olga were deemed joint owners of the
ranch. Tom's position was sacred and Olga couldn't be without
him – or me.

After a few months I could almost smell my new position
and the money. I knew I was close to hooking a marriage with
Olga Kelly. The lack of grief for Gus was a gift I cherished too.

Olga was proving to be more cautious than I'd thought she'd
be. She loved the bad boy in me and, of course, she thought that
she could mould me for her own purposes. I was also becoming
more sober, cleaner and mannerly. This was not because of her
– it was because of Tom's belief in a lost cause.

Olga is a clever woman – as plain women need to be. With a
fast-fading youth, her curves were getting fatter and she lacked
the beauty she saw on the screen. She had means and saw what
I did to Polly. Olga was right to be wary of marriage.

'You want to marry me to own this place?' she suggested one
day while we were outside on the front steps discussing the
needed repairs to the butchering house. 'Admit it.'

'It's a bonus I'd not throw away.'

'Do you love me?' she asked. In all the time I'd known her

this was a new question I wasn't prepared for. That slight hesitation ruined all my manipulations to that point. 'You don't care for me? You don't love anyone but yourself!' she said and walked off back inside. I wavered there on the steps. I knew that I should follow her. I never chased a woman (other than my Ella) and pride stuck me to the spot.

The money I was making and not spending was mounting up. Tom was generous and gave me commission on all new meat-packing contracts as well as my labouring wages on the ranch. I was not stuck for a few dollars and as I looked around the barns and the fields in the distance, I thought of the responsibility that came with being in charge. There would be a big noose around my neck.

The men made it easy for Tom. They listened and worked hard on his projects, they leaned on him for advice and rallied to support him. Would they do that for me? Unless I started mimicking Tom's personality, the way I'd done with Jock or the popular boys on the ship, all those years ago – I would have a large group working against me. Those thoughts made Hammy follow Olga up the steps.

She was in the kitchen at the long table made from a large oak we carted in from near the river. 'I find it hard to love anyone,' I told her. 'I lost the only two women I cared about. Now, I find it difficult to be close with others. You see that when I'm with the men too. I cannot let anyone know me. I don't make friends. It's a failing in this idiot you love.'

She listened and I thought of what Tom might do next.

'I saw Gus fall, Olga. I was glad that he died.'

That was the clincher. I had trusted Olga and revealed weaknesses. I had talked about my feelings and my past. Vulnerable, bad-boy Hammy was ready for a woman's love to change him.

'Let's get hitched?' I asked.

'I'll think about it,' she said. I was hopeful.

37

CHARLIE QUINN

It was hard to ignore the beauty of the Canadian landscape. It was still changing under the rule of the white man. We culled and pillaged and didn't listen to reason. Canada's flora and fauna was as hardy as the indigenous people – the prairie crocus or pasque flower litters the meadows and grasslands and the flow of clear streams is good for the soul. The change of weather from one day to the next still amazes me. Unlike Irish days where all the mild seasons appear in twenty-four hours, it is Canada's weeks that can swing from glorious hot sunshine to biting cold.

I came to love the wide-open spaces and beautiful scenery and thought less and less of my Ireland and the Ella-love I'd left behind.

'Men with ambition cannot think too much about the consequences,' Tom said, and I nodded at that. 'This war is taking too many good men. I hope that you're not still interested in enlisting?'

'I'd like to marry Olga.'

'I'm glad to hear it! You've both been fooling about for years.

Make her see sense and settle down. I'll have a quiet word with her as well.'

Tom's blessing meant a great deal to us both. I was sporadically staying in Olga's room again in the big house. We hadn't left a decent period for her to be a widow and didn't care. There was more and more mentions of Canadian military being sent to the British war. It wasn't popular with everyone, as thousands of badly-prepared men and boys were being sent and the casualties were high. Some poor sods refused to engage in the process. This got them the name 'Zombies' and much as I didn't want to go to war, I wasn't going to slink away from my duty either.

When nowhere near danger I am always brave.

Tom had suggested that his influence would keep me at home and safe. I wasn't to consider soldiering as it was mostly the young, unmarried and unskilled that were being conscripted. He was right.

When it came to preparing for another Christmas meal, I decided to try my luck with Olga one last time.

'Marry me.'

'Yes,' she said, and continued to peel the potatoes.

'A wedding in the new year then?'

She shrugged. There was a sense of purpose between us.

In June 1941 Randal Hamilton got married to Olga Kelly in the smallest church in Winnipeg. I never set foot in it before or after our wedding. We honeymooned in the cabin and took picnics out to the nearest of my favourite spots in the prairie.

As a naked Olga lay amongst the wild flowers and the glinting sunshine, I thought I was happy despite an invisible wound that couldn't heal. The flies, biting mosquitoes and ants were ignored, and we tried to make the most of the privacy.

I was now a man of means, property, land and prestige and the workhands didn't care. They weren't as easily won over as Olga. I couldn't use my youth and good looks on them. They weren't convinced that I deserved the position that I'd fucked and manipulated my way into. I wanted to be like Tom, and this was not coming quickly enough for an impatient Hammy.

Olga was busy too as a meat-producer and this was frowned upon by many. Without the tyranny of Gus she was thriving. I thought of Ella and my own mother and what a difference they might have made if they had Olga's opportunities. I could see that Olga was well fit for the mental stamina it took and she earned us a pile of money. I recognised and admired the driven ambition she had.

'I'll never hit you,' I promised her regularly.

There was no sign of pregnancies and although both she and I suffered from intestinal issues, like ulcers now and again, we were healthy and industrious.

With Olga away from the homestead most days working and travelling, the place needed the feminine touch and it was suggested to her at church that we should take in a home-child. It seemed children in need were still being shipped into Canadian ports, even with the war going on.

'NO!' I roared. 'Never!'

I hardly ever lost my temper with my Olga. The raised voice stunned her.

'Are they still sending children here? I saw them when I came. It made me mad to see them treated worse than cattle,' I said. 'Those poor children have a terrible time of it. I know that you'll tell me many have found loving homes. Many haven't. If we talk about them, we need to be offering them donations or a good home. I won't use them as labourers.'

I hadn't meant adoption, but Olga took it as such immediately. 'Could we take one in as our own?' she asked.

'Let me think about it.'

Bridget Fahy and the others from Daly's sat in my mind for many hours – maybe even for days. I thought about all the boys like Randal on the ship, all the slaves on ranches who'd starved or frozen to death, all of the stories I knew and all of the ones I didn't know. It was hard to believe that children were still suffering and I was still staying silent.

There was nothing to be done. Whatever way I turned it over, it was all hopeless. These children had nothing else in their lives at home. Like myself, they may have left more hardships behind them. I told myself that many were bound to be better off now in beautiful Canada. Who was I to say that all situations were like Daly's?

I grappled with how Charlie Quinn could leap out of the shadows, when things were finally settling into a nice future. I'd worked hard for the life I was living and I chose to ignore the truths I knew.

As per usual, I was a silent coward who turned his back on those who needed him.

I also said no to Olga's wishes to adopt. I had no right to ruin another child's life.

38

CHARLIE QUINN

A car pulls up at the house I'm staying in. A modern car for the 1990s that I should know the name of. It's not Canadian and I care very little about vehicles. Reluctantly, I learned to drive. A horse is a far better mode of transport. Even with my bad bones and health, give me a horse any day.

I press stop on the recorder and wait to see what fresh hell will come through the door.

'Charlie.'

It is Joe. Cheerful, boring Joe, whose main occupations are: accountancy, trapped fatherhood and grass-cutting.

'All alone?' he asks, looking around.

'I've upset Rhonda.'

'Really?' He places the shopping on the floor in the hall. Her eyes give out to him for leaving his things there every evening and I say nothing. 'It's usually me she's angry with.'

'Not this time.'

'Was it something you told her for the tapes?'

'Yes.'

'Oh dear.'

'I did say that it wasn't going to be all plain sailing.'

'You did warn her and she's easily upset sometimes.' Ordinary Joe shrugs his suited shoulders and pulls his tie looser. 'Gone to her mother's, I suppose?'

'That's what she said.'

'I'll call her in a while. I was looking forward to telling you both that I've got news.' If Joe could look very excited he was looking it now. Eyes agog, mouth wide, hands outstretched, palms facing upwards, stance open and animated. 'Ella wants to meet you.'

I sit forward in the chair.

'The public relations team, who is helping Ella, were very interested to know that you were back in the country. I was a little sketchy about your plans and details as I worry about these PR types. I asked for you to get to see her and they agreed. Unfortunately, it cannot be before Friday's interview. I did my best. They are to confirm a date and time.'

'Thank you, Joe.'

'Anyhow, if we make our way to Dublin, she and her... wait for it... PR team will arrange a meeting for this Saturday afternoon.'

'Team, eh?'

'I know. How crass! She's a convicted killer and she's got a PR company helping her improve her image.'

'And do they know about Rhonda recording me?'

'I didn't tell them anything really. I said I'd get back to them this evening, once we'd discussed things. I'll see what Rhonda thinks too, eh? She might have to ask the paper she's pitched to about exclusivity of your story.'

'Might she now?'

'I was impressed at the speed they all got back on. Once I got a number, they replied immediately when they heard your name. That's what swung it.'

'How is Ella?'

'Good. I think. Finds it hard to walk far but for her age she's in good health.'

'Not dying like me? Can I get to Dublin somehow?'

'Of course, I'll take you. I hate city traffic but we'll drive you down.' Joe washes his hands and beams a big smile back to me on the couch. 'Rhonda will be fine. She can have strange notions at times. She's been finding it tough since the baby. I'll talk to her. You've come a long way and after all this time, it's only right that you get to see Ella.'

'Thank you, Joe.'

'Tea or something stronger? Let's celebrate.'

'What is the something stronger? I like whisky.'

'Bushmills here we come,' Joe says, sticking his head into a cupboard. The sight of the brown liquid in the crystal glass brings a lump to my throat. The smell of it stings and the water rushing in to dilute the potency is a nice sound. 'I know I have to hear and understand a lot of your life, Charlie. Rhonda has been working hard in the evenings taking notes and making calls. I haven't had a chance to listen to any of the tapes. Are you doing okay with it all?'

'I'm fine thanks, Joe. Feel free to listen to some now. I might have a rest after I take my medication and pack my bags.'

Putting an old man in a downstairs bedroom was a good idea, as old legs cannot make the steep steps. I hear the recorder go on as I get my clothes from drawers, then there's the muffled voice of Charlie Quinn. I swallow the tablets and settle on top of the bed for a short sleep. I'm out for maybe an hour. My naps never last long, it is the cowboy in me. Brief snoozes are refreshing in the shade.

Returning into the corridor that leads to the kitchen and living room, I cannot hear any tape recording. There's a screech of a rewind and Rhonda's voice saying, 'I had Faye to keep Joe with me. I don't want it mentioned again.'

My shuffle towards the noise is long enough for Joe to have turned the volume up and have rewound the tape twice.

'I'm sorry, Joe. I forgot that was there,' I say when I can see his figure on the couch.

Joe puts his hand into his hair and pulls.

'We all have our reasons for secrets, lies and actions,' I say, lifting the crystal glass.

'Why did you come here?' Joe yells and makes me dribble my whisky. 'Why did I have to hear that?'

39

RHONDA IRWIN

There is a large package from Margie on the hall stand. I cannot face much more of her research. I don't know why it is affecting me this much. There's a sense that nothing will ever be the same again after Charlie's visit with us.

And as soon as I see Joe's face, I know there's something else wrong. He's sitting on the sofa with a whisky and there's no sign of our guest.

'I left Faye with Mum,' I tell him, hoping that I'm reading the seriousness of the situation wrong. 'She wanted to keep her for fish fingers and beans. There's been another delivery from Margie. Each one takes its toll on my time and I thought I'd get a chance to write something as Charlie didn't want any questions about his terrible revelations today. I need to talk with you, if you feel up to it.'

Joe turns his head in my direction and I hear him mutter, 'I listened to some of the tapes. All was fine until I heard your voice.'

Did he say he heard me on the tapes? I hold my breath.

'I listened to your revelation over and over. About Faye. About how you had her to keep me?' Joe says.

'Joe. I...'

'I couldn't figure out what had come between us.'

'It wasn't...'

'It wasn't what? What wasn't what, Ronnie? What have I missed all these months? Tell me.'

'I didn't mean for it to happen.'

'You didn't think I would find out? Or you didn't intend on getting pregnant? You didn't mean to lie? Which is it?'

'I don't know,' I admit. 'I don't know what to say.'

'Tell me the truth. You got pregnant on purpose and then made me feel guilty for it. You made me feel that it was me who ruined your life – our lives!'

'I have no words.'

'For love of Jesus, Rhonda! I blamed myself. I thought that I caused you to have your depression, that the pregnancy was the start of our problems, and it wasn't my fault at all.'

'I never knew that you felt guilty. I'm sorry,' I say through a sob. 'I just stopped taking the pill. It wasn't a big deal really. It was just an omission, a letting things take their course. A quiet lapse. I thought it would help us commit.'

'Commit? Commit to what?'

'To each other. You didn't see that I needed to move us on to the next level.'

'Move us on? For whom? Move us on to what?' He's on his feet striding, worryingly angry. Not like himself at all.

'For the look of things, for people to stop asking when we were going to settle down. To prove we were a couple.' I suddenly hear myself. It sounds fierce.

Joe's hands delve deep into his hair. He's in terrible despair. I've never seen him like this – ever. It's scaring me.

'I know you wanted to get married – but this? I loved you. I really loved you.'

40

CHARLIE QUINN

There's no sign of breakfast, baby Faye, Rhonda or Joe. I sense there will be no questions today. Tonight is Ella's interview and I have no way to get to Dublin. I doubt that Rhonda and Joe will sit into a car with me or each other.

I'm about to look for the phone directory to make an effort at getting my own way to the capital when Rhonda appears in a dressing gown. She's been crying. Her eyes are swollen and there's a red tip to her nose.

'I'll make us toast and coffee,' she says. It seems that Rhonda is ever the hostess. 'Joe heard too much yesterday.'

I nod. She's not looking at me.

'Is Joe here?' I ask.

'Of course he is. Joe is a man of his word. I told you that.'

The kettle clicks on and I watch the robin in the garden watch us.

'Why did you let him hear that?' she asks.

'It was unfortunate. He came home early and I didn't want to talk and I let him listen to the tapes. I didn't see any harm. He was all excited about getting me an appointment to see Ella. I suppose that was his reason for being home early? I'm sorry, Rhonda.'

'I don't know what to do.'

'Joe is loyal. Everything will be fine. And I sense my coming here will put things right in many ways.'

'Pah! You only talk about what suits you,' she says, banging mugs onto the counter. 'We've uncovered quite a bit, Charlie. Of course, you don't want to talk about that.'

She fills the kettle. This is a new side to Rhonda. She was fine with me being in control. Until now. I know she's upset and the facade she uses is slipping.

'I learned that at the outbreak of the war your father needed to go to hospital,' she says. 'He was getting dementia. "Starting to dote and be aggressive" I think was the term used to describe him at this time. Cedric paid for him to be cared for in a Belfast sanitarium. He rarely visited but Anna did and she kept diaries. Her family have been very helpful. They wanted to be good to you too. Anna's daughter copied some extracts from the diaries and sent them on to me. In short, Charlie, your father confessed to Anna that he killed your mother by drowning her in the barrel in the backyard. Why did you not tell me this?'

'Ah.' The twist in my gut clenches and it groans in hunger as I had no meal last night.

'I don't want to hurt you but it needed said. You're not shocked?'

'No.'

'Do you know what else it said?'

'My father would have said anything to Anna. She didn't remember him at his worst.'

'You know the rest, Charlie. I know you do. Your father made you help him. He insisted that you bring the cart around and made you haul and push your mother's corpse onto it. Then he pushed it, with your help, to the quarry and tipped her over the edge.' Rhonda holds her own throat in panic at saying that. 'Is that a lie?'

'I was a child.'

'Did he make you help him?'

'What do the diary accounts say?'

'It says that you cried and refused to do it. That you wanted to take off her apron and make her look pretty. Your father wouldn't let you and made you help him. I think that is the right version. You always thought of her apron, because he wouldn't let you take it off her. You poor thing, Charlie. This is terrible.'

A tear lodges in the corner of my eye and blots the glass on my spectacles.

'You were damaged by that alone,' she says sympathetically. 'You knew if you told anyone about it, Anna and Cedric would have been taken away. He threatened that you all would have no parent left and would be taken to the orphanage. You loved your mother and it was such a cruel start.'

'He was a righteous man and he got away with it.'

'I don't blame you for the way you are. Your little mind must have been scarred by an experience like that.'

'How did Father die?'

'In his sleep shortly after he was taken into the sanitarium.'

Rhonda has been doing a lot of poking into the past. I blow my nose and add, 'It's a pity he had an easy death. I always prayed that the bastard would die roaring.'

41

CHARLIE QUINN

The quiet couple, who have held commitment and secrets from each other, sit in the front seats and let me stretch out in the back. We are going to find Ella. Faye is left with a grandmother who I possibly met and who probably has heard of my sins now too.

I know both of these young cubs think that I am a bad person and I suppose that I am. They're not talking to me or to each other at the moment and this suits me fine. I want to speak to Ella before I divulge anymore. I should try to help them... I've already done enough and the silence is nice for the hours in the car.

The hotel is sparse, modern and shiny. My room is next to theirs and I can hear them argue. Lying on the purple, bobbled throw on the bed, the muffled annoyance disappears and a door bangs.

How is Ella today? Where is she? What is she feeling? Has she heard that I am going to see her soon? Does that make her as happy as it makes me?

She's in her eighties now. How might she look? Will I recognise her? Might she have aged better than I imagine?

I know that I'll still love her. Her beauty will remain despite the hardship of our years apart.

The country is awash with talk about the show. The barman and waiter both mentioned wanting to be near a TV later. Thankfully, Joe and Rhonda kept their information about me quiet and we ate silently. I sipped at the soup as Rhonda had grunted annoyance about the noises, and the liquid slithered down my acidic gullet to settle in with the pills. I'm nervous as I wait alone in the purple-themed room for *The Late Late Show* to come on.

There is the theme tune, the lights and compassionate host.

'Earlier today, *The Late Late Show* team recorded an exclusive interview with Ella O'Brien. Most of tonight's show is this exclusive report. For those of you who perhaps don't know, Ella gained notoriety when she was found guilty of three counts of infanticide in December 1931. She was later released from what was considered to be a lenient sentence to the care of the Sisters of Good Hope. It was felt that she got an easy reprieve as she always lacked remorse or understanding of her crimes. Ella O'Brien remains in the consciousness of the nation and this is her story. We wish to thank her for finding the time and energy to speak candidly. We've not heard from Ella herself and tonight she wishes to set the record straight. Ella has asked that following the interview, people leave her extended family and that of her late husband's family, or any other persons named tonight – in peace. Ella resides with the Sisters of Good Hope and she also wishes to remind the general public that she will not be answering further questions or doing further interviews. She wishes for the convent to remain a place of solace. After sixty years or more of silence, Ella reveals all that she knows to me now, in this sixty-minute interview. It is safe to say that the nation will be saddened and shocked by what she has to say.'

The camera leaves the host's face and pans around to an old, grey-haired woman in a chair. She is the woman I've missed and loved for this long.

'Ella O'Brien – welcome.'

'Thank you,' my Ella says without a smile or a gleam in those familiar eyes.

'We all feel like we know you. From all of the coverage over the years, we all think we know who Ella O'Brien is. Meeting you for the first time and listening to our researchers, I know that we do not know the real you at all. Why come forward now, Ella? Why talk now after all these years? Talk to us and explain your reason for granting us this interview.'

Ella touches her hair, just as she used to, and I let all the past go – all the angst sinks out of me as she breathes and looks into the camera.

'Many people have made their minds up about me and about what I did. People hate me. Loathe me. I seem to be a figure to demean and debase. I've had dreadful things sent to where I've stayed over the years. As you say, those listening think they know me. I felt that it was finally time for my voice to be heard.'

My Ella looks and sounds broken. A tired, wizened hand takes a heavy glass from the side table and shakes it towards her lips. Is this an act? Ella was never one for sympathy. She was tough as nails and unapologetic about her natural charisma. The nation must have cracked that veneer she possessed. That makes me sad. I gulp back tears. Is this all that is left of my Ella?

Someone out of shot takes the glass of water back and she thanks them.

'I understand that, Ella... why talk to me now after sixty years?' the interviewer asks again.

'You know why.'

There is the Ella I remember. The defiant gal who swanned

around the village making us lust after her. The camera focuses closer on many wrinkles and her drooping eyelids.

'You felt affinity with that case recently. You felt a need to speak up because of the recent coverage around an incident similar to your own? That young girl who gave birth and who was...'

'I wouldn't want to use anyone else's grief or situation for my own purposes. That is another person's pain, another person's story. I've no right to muddle into that pain. I'm not here to comment on that situation, other than to say that the coverage of this case has made me tired. It has made me cross, too, perhaps. We will never know what the real tale is, as no one is truly helping. People judge, they presume, they sit and half listen. They have no idea of anything. That is my point. That is what I've come here to say. Listen carefully and know all of the facts before judging any woman.'

'You have our attention. The nation is watching and listening.'

There's her indignant stare. Bravo Ella! 'That suits you well then, too, doesn't it?' she says at her host. 'I'm not naive enough to think that you wish to help me. This will all rise your ratings.'

The presenter looks stuck for words, toying with his pen. He looks flustered and gathers himself quickly. 'You know how to work things to your advantage, Ella. This has always been said about you. Is this true?'

'An Irish woman shouldn't be too pretty, too ambitious, too much of anything. It's always been that way. You don't like me as I'm too much for you to handle and manipulate. If I do work things to my own advantage that shows wit and intelligence – is that an evil thing? Are you trying to make me look bad already?'

'Are you a feminist, Ella? Is that what you are?'

Ella sighs and then touches the sweep of long hair going back into the golden clasp near that delicate ear. The style is old-fashioned now and it still suits her. 'For the love of Mick,' she says, gritting her teeth and dismissing the remark and looking at a notebook she takes from the side of the chair. Enthused by whatever is written on the paper, she takes a breath and says, 'For most of my youth I wanted to be liked, accepted and loved. No matter what I did it never seemed to happen for one reason or another. I was too beautiful. Yes, you can look like that if you like – I was a stunning-looking woman. I wasn't liked. I was too much; too harsh, too soft, too silly, too serious, the list goes on. People simply didn't like me and I tried to change who I was – to be liked, accepted and loved – and look where it got me.'

'The viewers will want us to say at this point, that this is not all about you. There were innocent babies involved. Three of your own children. Talk to us about them.'

'They are...' Her voice breaks. The host and the audience shifts uncomfortably. 'This is why I'm here, of course. You are correct. There is more to speak about. And I might be able to talk to you about my three, precious babies.'

42

CHARLIE QUINN

Reaching out from this uncomfortable chair, my fingertips touch the screen. I long to touch her hand. I'd squeeze it reassuringly and pat it to give strength now. My precious Ella is still there.

She closes us out with those eyes and is transported back to when I wasn't in her life.

'I met my husband when we were both young and foolish. At secretarial college I was rejected by the other girls, for being hard-working, glamorous and confident. I was all of those things, and also impatient and not very friendly. I was full of myself and possibly did need a large kick in the arse. Who doesn't at that age? The work itself and their chats about the future bored me silly. There was no incentive to do anything else other than land a good catch.

'To succeed I found the best looker, a trainee medical student and he was from a well-to-do family. I was punching above my weight, as they say. I knew he was infatuated and yes, I tricked him into marrying me. I had my reasons, and if women are honest, they still need to work things... how do you put it...? Work things around to our advantage. There was a great deal about him that was hidden too. I wasn't the only liar or bad person in the marriage.'

Watching Ella I can see all that I loved about her and my gut writhes around as I can also tell how this honesty might sound to those judging from their chairs at home.

'I thought I was in love – don't we all? I didn't know what love was then. Had no clue about what I was doing. Our families pretended to be delighted and we all ignored the bump in my expensive dress. The baby came way too early. Fully formed, though, it left me – and it was shocking how perfect the little thing was when the terrible pains left. Before you ask, I did nothing to harm the child, nothing to make him leave, nothing to hurt the innocence I had grown fond of. The child was still-born. It wasn't like I could ask questions, speak of it or find out what happened to the remains. Those many months and preciousness were swept away, like it never happened. That was it. Everything just went away – until it was needed to condemn me. I lost the baby and everyone wanted me to shut up, move on, smile and be resilient while listening to the gossip of how I snared a poor, gullible doctor.'

'Let's talk about your husband.'

'I know his name has been everywhere. I know what that does to a person and their family. He is dead now and I find it hard to speak ill of someone who cannot speak for themselves. I wanted to bring this forward before his death. I was advised against it. I listened and totally regret that now. He was supposed to speak up for me before it was too late. I should have known he wouldn't have done that. I've trusted the wrong people all my life.'

'What might you say to him if he were still alive?'

'I would laugh that he never got shot of me. Divorce isn't possible and – the poor beggar was stuck with Ella O'Brien. Even for him, that was a large cross to carry.' She laughs a little at the awfulness of her marriage. 'He beat me. I think most people around us at the time would've known that – if they were asked. They knew the battering I got regularly. I drove him to it. Everyone said that. I was made to believe that I was to blame. Those in the queue at the butchers would whisper that I was too thin and wiggled my bum too much when I walked. They said that the doctor was a respectable, professional man who had a harlot for a wife. It sounds silly now. It hurt. It made me into what they said I was. Lumbered with the lies, I became what they despised – to spite them.'

Ella doesn't look at the host or the audience for validation, she refers to the notebook, breathes deeply and resumes. She is still a fine woman. God! How fine she is.

'We never talked about our feelings in those days. If you asked someone how they were doing, you didn't really want to know how they were. There was no escape. No. I'm making excuses and going off the point. Maybe all of this is necessary. I want to explain my mind, how things were. I was intrigued by the way men responded to my looks. Even as a young girl, I knew that I had to let them leer because to complain was unpopular and silly. Them copping a feel was an endorsement. I was a success if men whistled or made lewd suggestions. It was a sign that I was valued. The attention was welcomed as it meant I was being accepted, loved and sometimes even adored. That's what I wanted most in this world – slowly I realised that this attention wasn't always a good thing. By then, it was too late. The damage was done. Even before my marriage, my reputation was sealed. I was what I was. There was no escape. My second pregnancy happened and no matter what has been said – the child was my husband's. He raped me. He did it often. It wasn't considered rape. It was in marriage, and that was what it was. He thought what he was doing was right and he made excuses for it. I know he didn't see his behaviour as disgusting or controlling –

but it was. I was hard to manage and I knew it. The whole village knew it. He was doing his best to do his duty. The baby came very early and didn't breathe either. Just as before all was swept away from me. There was little I could say or do. The numbness is difficult to describe. The lack of understanding I had for what was happening to my own body was huge. My brain and heart were broken and sure nobody cared about that.'

There's a stinging sensation behind the corners of my eyes when I press on them. I can hear Ella talk more about the village and the normality of traditions and religion. She's making a whole lot of sense. Bringing people into the places we lived. She's giving them a flavour of the old ways that are gone now and not long forgotten. Ella was always well-spoken and now is no different. How I've missed and admired her. The host mentions a commercial break and I listen to the advertisements about butter, computers and cars.

Then she's back with me. Her on one chair, me on another. We're nowhere close. Ella's nodding that she's ready to resume. I'm shaking.

'I let myself down. There were many women who endured all of this and much worse. Those fine women didn't let themselves or their families down. They didn't expose their little infants to the rigours of scrutiny or their own lives to the courts. If only I was more placid, more accepting, more moral, more like most women. I've learned now to accept my life and I fought against all of it for a very long time.'

'You brought this upon yourself? Is that what you are saying?' the host asks without the camera leaving Ella's eyes.

'I was no angel. I told you that. And yes, most of this is probably my fault.'

'You were tried in a court of law and found guilty.'

'I was guilty.'

43

CHARLIE QUINN

'I never spoke out at the time. I was in a terrible state. Even if I could have pieced together what had happened, I doubt anyone would have believed me and I doubt that it would have made things any better.'

'Speaking the truth would have made things worse?' the host asks Ella.

'Much worse. People in my once doting family had turned against me. I was a criminal woman. Even if my brain had functioned, I doubt I would have been restored to the woman I should have been.'

'The third baby. The trial. What do you remember of that?'

'Not much. I was heavily medicated and in pain in here.' Ella points to her head. 'I never spoke up. I tried to explain how he treated me, how I knew who hurt my baby. Nonetheless, it was me who was found guilty.'

Ella stops for a drink. It's excruciating waiting for that sip. 'In despair, I tried to hurt myself. That was it. I was unhinged, mentally unstable, a danger to myself and others. This was a sure sign of my guilt. The evidence of it laid out with the cuts I'd managed to do with something. All was sealed and delivered for justice.'

'You're saying you didn't do what you were accused of? That you didn't hurt your third child?'

'It wasn't me.'

'Then who?'

Ella shrugs.

'You're saying that it was your husband. The doctor?'

'I'm saying it wasn't me. The Sisters of Good Hope found me intriguing. One of them was doing studies on criminals, yes I know it is odd even now. There was one forward-thinking sister, and she asked for the notorious Ella O'Brien to be released into her care. Many of us female prisoners were. I think I might have disappointed her as time went on. I was not the criminal that people had made me into.'

'You said yourself you were guilty? What did you mean?'

'I was guilty of almost everything – but not the worst of it.'

'What you were sentenced for is rather brutal, Ella?'

Ella wrings her hands in her lap and she looks downwards. I reach out and touch her on the screen.

'I know,' she cries. 'I know.'

'Are you saying you weren't responsible for your actions as you'd lost your mind? That you weren't yourself at the time?'

'No!' she breathes heavily.

'Are you saying someone else did all you are accused of?'

Distressed now, her shoulders heave up and down in emotion. Mine mimic hers and she flops back a little into the chair. 'I had lost all sense of reality long before the last baby was born. I was not mad, though, if that's what you mean.'

'What happened, Ella?' His voice does sound concerned and also impatient. I want to punch him hard to stop him from hurting her. It feels like he is walking her into more danger. I want it to stop.

'Starved of real affection I found a kindred spirit. There was a young boy who worked in the butcher's.' She stops and looks straight at me. My heart leaps. It's as if she can see through the screen. 'He was a fine-looking fella, broad and strong. He had no decency in him either. I teased him and he gave me flattering looks and compliments. I was struck by his confidence and the beauty of him.'

'When was this?' she is asked. This lets me take a breath. I am weak now and trembling.

'I've no idea of the year. It was a long time before the baby and the trial. I wasn't a good woman, I wasn't a proper woman. I didn't care if I was corrupting a young boy.'

'Boy?'

'He was seventeen. Eighteen at the most. I was a married woman and had at least five years on him. He didn't seem that young to me, or to the butcher who employed him. The butcher always praised his abilities and gave him responsibilities. Like me, this boy tried to be accepted, to fit in. There was a counter between us and people watched our every move. So, for a long while, it was only my imagination that was silly and stupid. It was all safe then.'

Ella holds up her hand to stop the questions and takes some water to drink. Although her voice is the same it lacks the youthful tones she once had. What did I expect her to sound like after all this time? I want her to talk on and I also want her to stop.

'I encouraged him,' Ella says. 'I know it was wrong. As you made out I am not behind the door at manipulation and he had no experience. I was in need of his adoration. I didn't have to do much to have him following me around and asking my where-abouts. It was all ridiculous at the time. Sometimes my husband and I teased each other about infatuations boys and girls had. In the beginning I thought that this boy's interest might amuse him too – or make him jealous.'

I blink into the truth of her voice. Did she just say that they'd laugh at me?

'This young fella became fixated. There were jokes about it. Jeers when I went into the village. The butcher himself asked me to stop teasing the poor boy. I did stop and this didn't help the situation. I added to the mess as I visited him at his lodgings to try to explain my predicament. He suspected that I had feelings for him. I suppose I enjoyed the attention. He was attractive to look at and very immature. Despite what people thought – I was not a woman who slept around. I tried to explain that I was not a suitable woman for him. That enflamed his passions even more.'

'Didn't you tell someone?'

'Like who? And before you say my husband, I barely saw him and if I did he was trying to impregnate me. My family would have blamed me for flirting with the boy. His own mother was long gone and his religious father and nervous new stepmother did their best to discipline their unruly son. I suppose this young fellow was what you might call – a delinquent.'

My mouth hangs open and the tears stream into it.

44

CHARLIE QUINN

'This young fellow became my shadow. My family began to chaperone me most of the time. The rumours were piling up. It was not true what they said about my morals. I wanted to be a good wife and mother. In the finish that was the only job available to women. Being a conscientious, clever person, I wanted to succeed at those things. More than anything I needed to be the best at my role in life. A couple of times I tried to make my shadow understand this. He got frustrated and angry. I started to worry about what he would do.'

There's not a sound in the studio around Ella and not a sound in the hotel room next door. I've stopped crying and the toilet roll I've used to wipe the snot away is bunched at my feet. I stare at it. This is why I didn't want to hear from Ella. Inside, I must have known she thought these things.

'And what did he do to you?' the host asks.

Ella holds the nation's attention and pauses for many seconds. 'He seduced me and made me love him,' she says.

I look at my Ella. There she is, my darling Ella.

'I fell in love with a totally unsuitable boy. It was scandalous. I knew it was. His landlady frequented a public house. If she wasn't there, she was drunk, and then deaf and blind to what was happening in one of her rooms. I found love in those rare hours. Everything in me was screaming that it was wrong.' Ella grabs her skirt in two old fists. The pleats scrunch and she lingers like that a while, reminiscing about our lovemaking. 'He and I were seduced by each other. We were totally bowled over by the immorality, the danger and the thoughts of freedom.'

'You wanted to escape with this boy?' the host asks.

'I hate talking about my secrets like this. I hate having to share these private moments.'

'You wanted to run away together, is that it?' he asks.

'We talked about it. Emigration was high then too. We had no savings, of course. I wasn't allowed to have my own money and he made very little. I begged off my family when I thought they'd not tell my husband. Our pot of gold wasn't worth counting. I should've found a man with means to take me away and a couple of times I tried to end the lunacy. It wasn't long, though, until I missed him and went back for more love. He was...'

Ella cries into tight fists. The screen is smudged from me touching it. The host finds her some tissues.

What must the country think of her now? Do they empathise or still see her as a monstrous woman? We are all seeing her in pain and vulnerable. It's terrible.

'Can we go on?' she is asked. 'Can we ask about the third baby?'

'If we must. I hoped the baby was made in our love. The bump felt stronger this time and all was going fine. I was being left alone more. Everyone wanted to give this pregnancy a chance and I was happy.'

'What about this young man, what did he think?'

'When we did get time together I wanted him to myself. I didn't want to spoil the minutes with serious talks of responsibilities and lies. I suppose in my naivety I thought I could have him, the baby and my marriage. If I worked things well, I expected we could have it all. I could be a good wife and mother and still be connected to him. Don't we all want to have everything our own way?'

'Did this fellow want the baby?'

There's a hesitation and I shout at the screen. 'Answer him, Ella!'

'No. He didn't want the baby,' she breathes heavily then she tears up. More tissues. She dabs her cheeks. 'No. He didn't want the child. He wasn't stupid. He knew it might not be his and that the pregnancy would hamper our leaving Ireland. He never asked me to get rid of it. He knew how much I needed the child and he loved me enough. Or I thought he loved me enough.'

'You argued?'

'No. I was scared to argue with men. You might find it hard to believe but I'd learned being confident made men angry. It was easier to silently work on things behind the scenes. I thought I had it all worked out. Of course, I hadn't. It was while I was meeting quickly with my young love that the baby started to come. It was weeks early again and coming hard without much warning. Just like before. I was afraid. I left his lodgings without saying much. He knew I was in pain and that things might be imminent and most men didn't understand much about childbirth. I don't think women did either. I staggered home and got the neighbour's boy to run for my husband. It was all very traumatic. He gave me medicines. I don't know what they were. They were strong. He took the opportunity to make me suffer, berating me about what an awful woman I was and of how he knew about me and "the butcher's boy".'

Ella looks to the person sitting opposite her and then to the crowd. 'He was a doctor. A man people revered. Who was I? I remember my baby coming and then I woke to see love in one man's face and anger in another's. I told them both that I wanted to call her Maeve, after the great Irish queen. I don't know if I even got to hold her. Then all I remember is Maeve being gone and me being accused of awful things.'

'What men were there, Ella?'

'My husband and the love of my life, Charlie Quinn.'

45

CHARLIE QUINN

Ella is still talking. 'I did nothing to harm any of my babies. I have said this over and over. They were to be my job, my vocation. I wanted this child more than anything. My ambition was to be a better woman when Maeve was born. She was to be the catalyst for change. I couldn't have harmed her. I tried to make people listen. It was all I said. I didn't have the strength to articulate all of this other story then. Silence seemed better when I did surface from the trauma and unbearable sadness. The sisters came and took me into their fold. I was free in a way I didn't imagine. There were no bars or locked doors. Yet, I was unable to leave, not permitted to think for myself or to find Charlie. Minds were made up. People judged without the facts. My fate was sealed and there was no way back from what I was.'

'You pleaded guilty?'

'When you know that you're not an innocent woman, when you are told how vile you are every day, when you are rock bottom and there's nowhere to go, and all is lost, you don't care. I heard what was being said about me, and I thought I was something even worse. The butcher, Jock Daly, got word to me that Charlie had run off and then I was a totally broken woman. Parts of me still reek of the guilt that I deserved all of this. I had an affair, fell in love with someone other than my husband and could not be a good mother. I am conditioned to believe the worst about myself. I ran away in self-pity and fear.'

'Why now, Ella? Why tell us all of this now?'

'I saw that years haven't changed how things are. I hoped that time might change the world. People still aren't listening. There are always sides to stories that aren't seen or known. I am old now and unwell. With the help of good people, I felt it was time to speak up. It has taken me almost sixty years to find myself and my voice again.'

'And you wish people to believe you?'

'People believe what they want to. I've seen over these long years that sometimes talking makes things worse. Despite this, before I died I wanted, no, I needed to say that I did nothing to harm any of my children.'

'Who do you think was responsible?'

'This is frustrating. That is exactly what I'm trying to say to you all!' Ella points at the audience and the camera. 'I don't know what happened. I simply don't know. I wish that I knew for sure. I can guess. I can surmise and that is all it would be. Conjecture. We have no proof. I wish I'd had the strength years ago to ask, to force the truth out. I wish I'd had the belief in myself to fight.'

'After all this time you must have some idea about what happened?'

Ella sighs and holds her forehead.

'You surely must have someone you blame? Someone who took your good name and freedom from you?'

'I don't want anyone to blame.'

'Are you not angry? For sixty years you've been labelled as one of the worst criminals in Ireland. Let us be totally clear here,

Ella. Are you saying that you are totally innocent of the three counts of infanticide?'

'I am.'

There's my defiant Ella. How gorgeous is she?

'What happens now?' the host asks Ella as much as the production team in his ear.

'I want it to be known that I'm not an evil woman. I had such a terrible time with a cruel husband that I had an affair with a boy, five years younger than me. My babies were all stillborn. I was branded a criminal for my entire life, ruined, locked in a convent, questioned and spat upon. My own family walked away. I cried alone for years. My husband was never doubted – the whole place adored him. Thought he was the victim. No one will ever understand how it felt to be vilified. Hated. I lost everything – even my own name. Nobody cared. Over the years, one sister in the convent, who wants to remain nameless, helped me. With her guidance the younger members of the O'Brien family came to visit me and they have helped to bring all of this about. They've tried to make amends for a man who died last year with no remorse. I want to thank them.'

Ella pauses and then says, 'Nothing much has changed because tonight I still will go back into that convent. I'll do my few hours of office work tomorrow and I still crochet a little... I want to be heard and therefore I'm grateful that this has happened. And before I go, I want to ask people not to judge. There are always things we don't know. Live your life by being kind and good to others. Do not judge people. Thank you for listening to me this evening. May God bless you all.'

Ella goes to rise off the chair and a hand comes to hold her elbow and she is led off the set. The show rolls into a commercial break.

I wait for the couple next door to barge in and confront me after knocking angrily on my door. No. They don't contact me. I presume they've made up their minds about Charlie Quinn and who could blame them?

I lie back on the bed fully clothed and think about how Ella might be tonight. At least she is safe and heard now. That is all that matters.

The show returns with the host summarising Ella's words. 'What do you make of it, folks?' he asks. 'Should we be judging her now, when she asked us not to? An interesting conundrum. I think that we'd all like to know what happened to this fellow, Charlie Quinn. He is possibly the only one who can give us the answers we all crave. If we believe Ella O'Brien's tale then there are more questions than answers this evening.'

46

RHONDA IRWIN

As the nation reels from Ella's revelations, Joe and I are spiralling out of control too. He is slipping further and further away. He is silent and brooding. There's nowhere to escape in the hotel room and although the chairs are at a distance with beds between us, I feel his anxiousness before, during and after the television show. I rise to make us tea, or to at least do something. He's watching me, like Charlie does.

'What do you make of that?' Joe asks.

'Margie sent over papers and in the middle of some letters was one from Ella O'Brien to Charlie's sister, Anna. I have all of them in the car. I will get it and show it to you.'

'She's making out that it was either our Charlie or her husband,' Joe says. 'You've always felt Charlie's been hiding some-thing but I think she was trying to say her husband was to blame.'

'Charlie's been very honest and open about his worst thoughts. I think he would have told me if he is to blame for Ella's imprisonment. I dunno, though, why he's reluctant to say any more until he talks to Ella.'

'Do you think he knows more?'

'Yes. That's the way it seems.'

'Feck.' Joe sighs out long and low. 'It must have been hard on you to listen to those awful things every day. I'm exhausted after that there.' Joe stands and throws the TV remote control onto the bed. 'Like, what crimes did he admit to?'

'It didn't bother him to watch a man die because he wanted to take his wife and ranch.'

'Jesus!'

'I'm also wondering if he killed more people, Joe. Like Randal Hamilton, whose name he stole? There's also a little girl on a Canadian farm. I cannot stop thinking about her. I kept a close eye on Faye but I also took her to stay at Mum's a few times – just in case.'

'What?' Joe asks, his face concerned, his eyes wide.

'My mind is in such a mess.'

'Do you hear what you're saying, Ronnie?'

'We were good to him. He cannot be a monster. Joe – I'm sorry.'

Joe kneels down on his hunkers beside my chair. The kettle boils and clicks off as he takes my hand.

'He cannot be a monster,' I murmur.

'It's going to be all right. We're safe and Charlie cannot hurt anyone else now. He wants to make things right. I think that's why he's here. I doubt he hurt anyone.' He touches my cheek and smiles. 'We'll be okay, won't we?'

'I hope so.'

'I don't want to listen to much more. Maybe, while we drink this tea, tell me some of what is on the tapes. I'll go down and get the packages from Margie. Let's get some sort of handle on what is going on with this Charlie Quinn.'

When Joe returns with my briefcase full of papers I know exactly where the letter from Ella O'Brien is. I root it out of the pile and unfold it carefully. My hand trembles as Anna Quinn's must have when she opened it.

Dearest Ms Anna Quinn,

Thank you for your kind letter. I was glad to get any communication. It was extra special to get such a lengthy letter from someone who knows where I grew up and spent a great deal of my freedom.

You were a young girl when I saw you all those years ago and I am sure you've grown into a fine woman. Your mother was a stunning-looking woman and if you are anything like your brother, Charlie, people will stand in the rain to look at you.

It was nice of you to worry for my health and well-being. Not many have taken the time to be kind over the years. I was also heartened to read that you would keep our communication private. As you can imagine, some unscrupulous people would love to read a letter from an infamous criminal. I trust you to keep your word.

Please understand that I cannot write regularly, like you asked.

I know that you will not be aware that I knew your brother Charlie well. He worked in Daly's butchers and I had a great fondness for him. I enjoyed listening to his tall tales. From your letter, I sensed that you were alone in the world now, as I am. You mentioned losing both your brothers and it saddens me to think of Charlie being gone. Perhaps you might reply and let me know what became of him? I would dearly love to know. I heard that Cedric was a fine man too.

It is hard to be left, as you yourself say, alone and childless in the world. I felt we were kindred spirits in many ways and perhaps even if I don't reply, you might send me an occasional letter? I get very lonely. Many believe that I deserve such punishment. From your words, I sense a humanity that sees past maliciousness.

It was a nice surprise, too, that your letter arrived on what would have been the birthday of my last child, Maeve. I also took this as a sign that I should write back to Charlie's sister.

Anna, you have many questions. I know that you didn't ask outright if I am guilty of the crimes assigned to me and I felt you wished for me to confess or confirm my innocence. I cannot comment on the case for obvious reasons. I am not believed and this is hard to take. Writing to you comes from a deep loyalty to your brother. I sense that Charlie would like me to return your kindness.

If I told you all that I knew, I fear that it would only sully the nice memories you've already shared with me. As you are now a nurse, you will understand more than most. Nature doesn't always allow life.

I am not blameless but I did not and would not smother my babies. People don't listen. As you are Charlie's sister and your letter came on such an auspicious date, I need you to believe me.

As you are unmarried, you might not appreciate the complexities of such a union. You may not fear the wrath of a jealous husband, and I hope that you know the joy of true passion and love. Sometimes, Anna, when these crash into our lives, it is the innocent that are harmed the most. That is all I can say.

Someday the truth will come out and I just hope that it's within my lifetime. I would dearly love more letters, if you felt able to write to me. Please understand that I cannot reply again. Your family would be very proud of the kind woman you've become. I just wish that your brothers were here to see it.

You asked about my time with the Sisters of Good Hope. There is much to say about my life and don't we all have trials and tribulations to overcome? I am sure you have many too.

Due to some good sisters here, I've had a bed, good food and shelter and through some of them I've learned to have faith. A better world awaits us where we will be surrounded by all those we love again.

Yours in quiet truth,

Ella O'Brien

'Were there more letters?' Joe asks.

'I'm sure they sent all they had.'

'What Ella doesn't say seems most important. It was very good of Anna's family to keep this letter secret.'

'I don't think they knew they were in Anna's things. It was just another letter until they really looked into Anna's diaries. I don't think anyone read them before or knew that she wrote to *the* Ella O'Brien.'

I take time re-telling the tapes in summarised form to Joe. He leans in to peck my cheek.

'It's awful,' I tell him. 'So much isn't talked about at the right time. Things are left unsaid until it's too late. All that mattered to Ella was taken away and...' I'm crying again.

Joe's voice shakes as he says, 'We're going to be okay.'

As I close the curtains in this hotel room, I wonder about all that isn't said between us. It feels like nothing will be right, ever again.

47

CHARLIE QUINN

Breakfast is a self-service. When I shuffle in, the waitress offers to bring whatever I'd like. The badness in me wants to tell her my name rather than my room number. A reaction would make it all real, rather than the nightmare that it is. I'm always an early riser, having used the sun as a guide rather than a clock. The white, clothed tables are mostly empty.

When I return to my room there's a note under my door from those relations of mine. *We will take you to Ella at eleven o'clock. See you in the foyer at 10.55.*

They don't want to talk to me. I can imagine why they don't. Criminal Charlie Quinn is not deserving of conversation anymore. They believe that I'm a child killer.

There's not much on the television about last night's interview. The children's programmes and news are full and I'm curious as to how things have fallen. I'm walking to and fro, checking my jaws often to make sure I've shaved off all of the whiskers.

At 10.30 I brush my teeth again and fix my tie tighter, and pull lint off my knee. The radio by the bed is playing old classics.

I don't want to think of anything and the music helps sooth the nervousness.

At 10.45 I start my toddle to the elevator. I should've refused to use it when I came to the hotel. The stairs are impossible but I don't want to be demanding. Thankfully, it is spacious and gleams in mirror and chrome and moves quickly. My stomach heaves as I wait for the pins, pulleys and mechanism to take me closer to the inevitable.

The cupped red seats in the reception area are empty. Deciding how to get in and out of them must take a few minutes of agonising away as I am only scooped into the leather when I spy a red-faced Rhonda.

'Joe will be down shortly,' she says, holding out a hand to help me up. 'We promised to take you to see Ella.'

'Get me a taxi. I am going to be late.' I sound bitter.

'We don't like Dublin traffic, that might be a good idea.' She looks at me, and there is fear in that face. 'Yes, I'll ask reception to get you one.' Going to the desk she points back at me and talks to the lady.

'It will be five minutes,' Rhonda says to the top of my head. 'We should go with you.'

'I'd rather go alone, please. If Ella allows it I can record some of the conversation.'

Rhonda's expression brightens. The writer's brain takes over from the human one. 'I'll get the recorder. Wait on me to go upstairs. That's a good plan. Thank you.'

The taxi comes and Rhonda bundles me into it with another lie, 'I hope it all goes well for you, Charlie.'

48

CHARLIE QUINN

The PR company's offices are fancy. Leather, chrome and pinkish feminine shades of paint. I suppose it pays to help people present the best side of themselves. How are the nuns paying for such things? Why are they doing this for Ella? Randal Hamilton and Charlie Quinn could do with them. Ella has influential people protecting her now – I am glad of that. She deserves it all.

There's a young chap with acne waiting to help me find the office I'm needed in. He holds my arm and smells of chewing gum.

'No lifts! I don't do small spaces.' I stall near the shiny metal doors. 'No stairs.'

He tuts a bit and drags me after him. It's a long, painful march to a far-flung open-plan conference room. The place is teeming with people and noise. Some are wearing headsets and are pointing in various directions and some are moving chairs and lights.

All activity stops when we stumble into the room. Exhausted already, I must look like I might keel over as the chap gets a rollicking and I get an uncomfortable chair shoved under my backside. There's a perfumed air to the room and I spy fresh doughnuts on a trolley a good distance away. My tummy growls and I'm offered coffee.

'A doughnut,' I whisper and point pathetically.

'Your eyesight must be all right then,' the chap jokes.

'Your manners aren't,' I shout at him. People look over. I want to leave. I know from the activity that this is much more than a small gathering. Meeting my Ella was to be a private thing. This is circus-like. 'Who's in charge?' I ask.

'You must be Mr Charlie Quinn? I've been looking for you,' a lady with the nicest dark eyes says and she holds out her hand to shake mine. 'Ella will be right down. This is all for a press conference later. Don't worry. You've been taken to the wrong place.' Those beautiful orbs roll upwards in annoyance. 'Interns never listen.'

'He wouldn't go upstairs, I didn't know what to do. Did you say Charlie Quinn? I was just told Mr Quinn, I never dreamt that it would be you!' the acne-laden chap says, giving me a coffee and a doughnut. 'Like from the telly last night? You are *the* Charlie Quinn?'

'The very one.'

'Christ!' He backs away.

The nice lady doesn't move, smiles and rolls her eyes again. 'Won't be long now, Mr Quinn.' She pats my shoulder and looks towards the door I came in from.

The coffee and doughnut are long gone. The people are almost set up as they are filtering away, like my patience. The door swings open and a wheelchair is pushed into the room. Sitting upon it, regal, like the Queen of England, is my Ella.

I rise as best I can to greet her. She nods and then helps the nice lady to settle the chair in as close to my chair as possible.

'I cannot run away anymore,' I joke at them both. It was wrong to be flippant, and it is said now. 'I'm sorry. That wasn't meant to be the first thing I said. It wasn't even funny.' I gulp. 'Ella, I'm sorry.'

Those eyes are the bravest I've ever seen. 'What are you sorry for?' she asks.

'I came back to put things right, and it's been too long. I abandoned you when you needed me most. I'm sorry.' This speech is not coming as well as I would like. The sobbing is uncontrollable and embarrassing. Thankfully, there are not many in the room now. I'm making a spectacle of myself. An old man crying is disgusting. I manage to breathe and say, 'I've thought about this moment for sixty years. I've missed you. My life has been empty. I promised to make you happy and I let you down. I've had this conversation with you many times in my dreams and it was never like this.'

'It's good to see you, Charlie. Don't blame yourself. You were young,' Ella says. 'I should never have involved you in my life. You were unstable.'

This stalls my breathing and thoughts.

'That word is harsh I know,' she says. 'I've been studying over the years and I know now that you were suffering more than I was. The following me about, the neediness, the vulnerability. I was older and shouldn't have taken advantage of you.'

I want to touch more than her hand but the distance between our knees is too great for an old man to stretch over. I'm tense and in despair.

'You said last night that I was the love of your life?' Tears fall onto my lap. 'You said other cruel things – the one I remember most was that – you loved me?'

'I said that and it was true.'

'Was? I hoped that you might still love me. I love you still,' I whisper, leaning in as much as I dare on this shit chair. 'I have always loved you. It was only ever you.'

'Dear Charlie.' She holds her throat. 'They tell me that you are not well.'

I touch my stomach. 'Cancer. I'm being eaten away with guilt and loneliness.'

'You always could manipulate me.' Ella smiles. It is weak in its delivery.

'I didn't mean it like that,' I urge. 'I'm trying to say that I didn't get off scot-free from all that I did.'

'Tell me what exactly you did? I've imagined many scenarios over the years. Dreamt many variations. What kept you away? What kept you from me?'

'I ended up in Canada. I got stuck there and couldn't come home. I didn't have it easy and I made some more bad decisions.'

'Why doesn't that surprise me?'

'I tried Ella. I did.'

'And this is why I didn't want to know why you left. It's never your fault. Never.'

'You didn't want to know what happened to me?'

'If you couldn't come back, or let me know where you were, or what happened between us, then perhaps it was better that I didn't know it all. Safer not knowing.'

'Here we are – you agreed to see me?' My stomach twists in pure agony and I grit my false teeth together.

'They told me to meet with you. They said that you might help us get to the truth. They said that you might be here to put things right.'

'I have always wanted to help you.'

'Help me now, Charlie. Help me now.'

49

CHARLIE QUINN

With the tape recorder between us on a low coffee table, and me holding Ella's hand, I go back to Tyrone and the day Maeve was born.

'I've never told anyone this before. Not even Rhonda Irwin who I've been staying with and talking to. I've never said this before. I barely acknowledged it myself. I was frightened and I cowered outside your house. I now admit that I followed you to make sure you got back to someone who knew how to get babies out. I was late for work and I listened for as long as I could. The things he said to you were vile. He shouted and you were in such pain. I was sure that I'd be seen there and I snuck inside. I wasn't planning on confronting the doctor. Even with all my confidence, he was who he was, and I was just a butcher's boy.

'For a long time, I listened, shaking in the corner of some store cupboard. Then I couldn't hear anything for ages. I peered out and thought I heard the cry of a baby. Our baby. There was no noise from you or him and I couldn't stay where I was. As I got to the bottom of the stairs I sensed something wasn't right and for once Charlie Quinn ran forward and did the right thing. You were there lying on the bed, all wet and bloodied, with a baby in your arms. He was between your legs and you looked sleepy and unfocused. I wasn't sure if you could see me. Then you said, "Let's call her Maeve". I nodded, hoping he was too busy to notice me. You held the baby up and said, "Charlie, let's call her Maeve".

'Frozen to the spot, I tried to peer over the blanket from a distance. By then he knew I was there. I waited seconds for him to attack. Instead, he finished whatever he was doing, and you closed your eyes. The baby wasn't making a sound and the time was endless as I waited – for what, I didn't know. Wiping his hands, he stood up and approached me.

'"Coward – that's what you are", he said up close at my ear. "You foolish fucker! This baby is dead too. She killed it. Just like the rest. Run now, boy, before I say that you helped her do it".'

With the past gone, I turn and search Ella's face for belief; in me, for love, for forgiveness. There's none there.

'I ran, Ella. I turned on my heels and ran.' I use my sleeve to wipe the wet from my cheeks. 'I left you and our child. Say something?' I plead.

'Did you see her?'

'Maeve? Not really. I thought she had no hair and maybe dark eyes. Don't all babies look like that? In my dreams she was beautiful. I'm sorry. I ran away like a stupid boy. You believe me?'

'You were young and afraid,' Ella says, intently staring. 'After all this time you would tell me the truth.'

'Didn't you always know that? Did you doubt me that much?'

'I never thought you would hurt Maeve – but, you thought that I was the guilty one.' She sits back to see my reaction fully. 'Some part of you does. You must have wondered if it was true what he said about me? You didn't come back to help me – you felt I did what my husband accused me of.'

'No,' I whisper. 'You weren't capable of anything like that. You were weak from the birth and there wasn't enough time for you to do anything. I ran up the stairs after I thought I heard the baby cry. You were so weak but happy. There's no way you had the wherewithal to smother our child... and he lied to me, Ella. He told me that you'd hurt her, but she must have been alive then. I should have known you couldn't have done that. He threatened me and I was scared.'

Ella is crying now, dabbing her pain away with a cloth handkerchief from up her sleeve.

'I'm sorry,' I mumble, incapable of more.

'I prayed that you would stay away. I knew that if you came back you'd make things worse,' Ella admits with a sniff. 'You were always one for telling tall tales and you'd drag up our affair and make it look like I had even more motive. Or worse still, you would have incriminated yourself. There was such hatred for me. An affair with a young boy would have made things a million times worse. I didn't want you caught up in all of that even if you told them the truth – what difference would it have made? He was a "great man", I was a mad harlot and you were a young boy. Maeve was gone and we were never going to be the same. It was good that you left.'

'You wanted me to stay away? Jesus, don't say that,' I plead.

'You did stay away and you didn't come back.'

'I've been telling the lady who owns this recorder all about my life. Our time together.' I stop to check the machine is turning. 'It's a long tale, and it explains the awfulness that kept me from coming home to you. I said it all out so that you could listen and hear it. I wanted to explain what happened to prevent me from helping you. I need you to know what stopped me from remembering my past for all these years. You must listen to the recordings. Or maybe you could read what Rhonda is going to write. I want you to know it all. Want you to know me. There were circumstances beyond my control and mistakes I made which all kept me from you.'

Ella smiles sweetly. 'I'll hear what you have to say. I asked for people to do that for me. It is the least I can do for you.'

I click off the machine.

'I didn't tell the tapes everything though,' I say to Ella. 'I wasn't sure what you might remember or what you'd say in your interview. If you want me to lie for you, I will. If you want me to say that I killed our baby, I will. If it makes things better, I can lie. I love you that much – I'll say whatever you need me to. I'm dying, Ella and while I have the strength I'll say whatever I can to make things better. I can take the blame. I'll lie and tell them that I witnessed the doctor murdering our baby. He was there when I left you both. It was him. I know it was. I can do whatever you need me to. It's not fair that he lived a blameless life, doctoring and travelling the world. Tell me what you need me to do. We can run the tape again and I can say whatever you like.'

Ella gazes at me and says with a long sigh, 'You haven't changed a bit, Charlie. You're still the same.'

50

CHARLIE QUINN

They need to move the old couple in the corner. There is a press conference about the latest scandal. Thankfully, it isn't about us.

Ella's voice is firm. 'We don't need any more lies. We both know who killed our child. It wasn't you or I. It could only have been him. We have no proof though. I never had any. I'm used to that. All that we can say is what you know for sure. You didn't see him murder Maeve. I didn't see him do it either. We cannot lie. You cannot lie, Charlie. All I ask is that you tell the truth. Goodbye,' Ella says and leans on the arm of the wheelchair and sighs again. The nice lady comes to push Ella away as I clutch a piece of paper with an address and phone number she presses into my palm.

'Goodbye,' Ella whispers. 'No more lies, Charlie, no more running.'

'I love you,' I mouth as Ella is wheeled away. She waves. I'm alone. If I had paid heed to how I was brought in I might have found my way out. My breathing is heavy. I manage to get lost in a set of narrow corridors and spy the metallic shine of a lift.

Panicked, I vomit all over my new jacket. The floor sinks downwards.

There's a commotion about the elderly gentleman who had a turn and needs an ambulance. I start to explain that I am claustrophobic and have been through a lot. Then I realised hospitals have beds and nurses. The hotel isn't booked for another night and Rhonda and Joe aren't hospitable anymore. I groan and lie back into the floor and bad Charlie Quinn or Hammy waits on an ambulance.

I was whisked to a ward and seen by a doctor before the day was out. Being in a ward with four other doddery men doesn't bother the cowboy used to tents, bunks and snoring companions. The nurses are pretty. I'm comfortable, until there is a news bulletin on the national station.

'Charlie Quinn, mentioned in the Ella O'Brien interview last night, is said to have returned to Ireland after many years abroad. Charlie Quinn was the young lover of the infamous Ella O'Brien at the time of her arrest. There have been reports that Mr Quinn met with Mrs O'Brien today at an undisclosed location. It is hoped that he will explain what he knows about this case. When asked why Mrs O'Brien did not disclose this meeting, her representatives said that it was a last minute get-together and Mr Quinn has no further bearing on the case. In further news...'

Rhonda and Joe are alerted about the ambulance because they arrive to the hospital upset and concerned that I'm about to die on their watch.

'Please go home to Faye,' I tell a distressed-looking Rhonda. 'I don't want to burden you both further. The only thing I would like is to keep the recorder for now and ask you to make copies of the tapes for Ella? I'll let you know how I'm doing and what's happening.'

'Will you see her again?' Joe asks. 'How did it go?'

'Not very well if he ended up in hospital,' Rhonda says sharply.

'What do people think of all of this?' I ask. 'I notice you didn't tell the staff here. You let me be Randal Hamilton.'

They look at each other.

'They are willing to look after me until my blood pressure is back to normal and someone has spoken to my consultant on the telephone.'

'What did you tell Ella?' Rhonda says. 'During that interview, she felt that you knew something?'

'I hope I gave her the answers she needed. I told her and the tape recorder all that I knew. I'll send that tape and some more on to you soon. I want to speak with the police and with Ella again. We got rushed at our last meeting and I ended up in this spot of bother. Ella has given me contact details, I'd like to visit her again.'

'Of course.' Rhonda pats my arm awkwardly. 'They want to keep you for a few days.' She is relieved. 'When is your flight home?'

'I'm not even thinking that far ahead.'

'Let us know how you are,' Joe says. 'We must go, though, the parking will cost us a fortune.'

Poor, practical Joe. I smile, shake his moist hand and thank him. Rhonda air-kisses my cheek and they pull back the garish curtain from around the bed and leave. The lid over the scrambled eggs is shiny and I look at the reflection in it. 'Well, Charlie Quinn, you bad fucker, what is the next step?'

51

RHONDA IRWIN

'Why is he guarded about that one thing? Why is it that he will talk of other awful happenings and not the death of his own child? Why won't he help her now? He's come all this way. It makes no sense, unless he is the guilty one?'

Joe's driving is always careful and he hates when I start important discussions on the new dual carriageways.

'Is it awful of me to be relieved that he's in hospital and not our responsibility anymore?' I ask the side of Joe's head. 'I miss Faye too. I cannot wait to see her.'

Joe smiles and fixes his hands on the steering wheel. 'What do you think about it all? About Ella? About what happened?' he asks.

I sit and watch the greens of the hedgerows haze and focus over and over and want to make a conclusion as to how I feel about Charlie Quinn.

'I shouldn't like him, but I do. There's something endearing about Charlie, despite it all. I still do have a soft spot for him.'

'I'm glad it's almost over,' Joe says. His glance shows definite thoughts. I should ask him his feelings. As usual, I don't want to go into the hole in case I cannot come out. He takes a deep breath. 'He's still keeping secrets. We all know how unhealthy that is.'

'Why won't he say what he knows about Maeve's death?'

'He wants Ella to tell him what to do. He wants her permission, wants to make sure that he doesn't let her down again. I can understand that.'

'You don't let me down,' I reassure.

The traffic slows.

'We all have to try to make amends,' I say eagerly, watching for a reaction. 'We need to find each other again and make things better.'

Joe is silent and the brake lights of the car in front are very bright in the twilight.

I don't breathe and wait. There's nothing coming back. 'For Faye's sake too,' I go on, 'we should try to make things better between us?'

The car stops and idles in a long line of traffic. 'Shit! What's the hold up now?' Joe raises his chin and attempts to see around the car and lorries up ahead. 'We could do without this.'

I silently wonder if my mother would take Faye and I in. It would be an alternative place to live – if I could stomach her disappointment at me being an unwed, abandoned woman. Minutes in my brain are spent packing; locating suitcases, all the paraphernalia that I'll need for Faye. I have some cash. The thought of leaving Joe's solid dependability sinks home. I cannot imagine my life without him. Does he not want to fight for our love at all? Will he not speak and save us? Should he not try to patch up things for the family's sake? The side of his head is unchanged and I've been to hell and back in this silence beside him. I should scream but I am tired and weak.

'What did you say, darling?' Joe asks, looking over at me. 'I was miles away. Sorry. What did you say?'

'Can we make up?'

'I thought we had. Did we not sort things out this morning?' He raises an eyebrow. That quick, tense and awkward shag this morning was his idea of a reconciliation. It had been a while since we were intimate and that was his quiet ritual of him making amends while I imagined I had stale breath. 'I know it's been a while' – he winks – 'I thought we were back on track. All is good again, thank God.'

'Just like that all is forgiven? Forgotten? You've made up with me?'

'Ah. Things are moving now,' Joe says with a sigh. 'We'll be home soon.'

52

CHARLIE QUINN

I can sleep on a rock if I need to even though resting isn't easy for the other men on the ward. There have been questions about me too and the reason for my admission. I'm used to hiding my business.

All is fine until a visitor with a tabloid newspaper under their arm approaches my bed and asks, 'Are you Charlie Quinn?'

I deny it automatically and he points to the photograph on the front page. It is a close-up photo of Ella and I talking in the conference room with the PR company.

'All old men look alike.' I turn my back to him.

'It says here that Charlie Quinn has a slight Canadian accent and that he was admitted to hospital yesterday?'

I try to pull the curtain around and ignore the nosey fecker. The intern chap with a camera got paid properly for his time or perhaps Ella's protectors are looking for a scapegoat.

'Do the hospital know who he is?' I can hear the man ask my neighbour in the next bed. 'Do the Gardai know he's here?'

With the mention of police, I think that it is time to hobble to the nurses' station. I announce to anyone who can hear, 'I'm the Charlie Quinn from the Ella O'Brien story. I think you better phone the police.'

In a couple of hours I'm in a private ward in the hospital talking into two recording devices. I've rejected a lawyer. I know they are the worst crooks of all. The policemen are gentlemanly and kind as they ask me to state my name for the record.

The first few minutes is all about the fact that I have told great swathes of this tale already and that I will co-operate with them in every way. I explain that Rhonda and Joe are helping me and only know what I've told them in recent days. I promise that the police will have copies of the tapes I've already done. The men nod and ask if I feel up to some questions considering I've been admitted to hospital only twenty-four hours before.

'I have always been a scoundrel. You must understand that before we begin. I am dying of cancer. That much is true and from when I was a child I've been claustrophobic. When I passed out, I was in need of a place to "hide out" and I thought the hospital was as good a place as any. My hosts were tired of me, possibly scared and...' I slap the table. 'Here I am.'

'Why do you think you should speak with us?' one of the men ask me. 'Have you been in trouble with the law before, sir?'

'Never.' Then, I stop and think a moment. 'I have never been questioned by lawmen before now. No. Never.'

'You should have been questioned or arrested? Is that what you mean?'

'It's a long story.'

'And it's all on the tapes you mentioned?'

'Yes.'

'And once we listen to these tapes, you'll answer any questions we might have?'

'Of course.'

'You mentioned a lady called Rhonda. We've spoken to her and she confirmed that she's helping you record all of this information and she summarised some of her concerns for us.'

'Oh.'

'She said there were old crimes, very old crimes, on the tapes and in her research. She's discovered that you were involved or present at some murders and deaths?'

'That's right.'

'And that you never spoke about them until recently.'

'Also correct.'

'These include...' He looks at a notebook. 'Your own mother in County Tyrone, a young orphan girl called Bridget Fahy in New Brunswick, Canada, and the first husband of your wife in Manitoba, Canada? There are concerns, too, for a lad you assaulted and stole from and now impersonate called Randal Hamilton.'

'That's a long list. Yes, I think Rhonda was concerned for what happened to them as well.'

'And there's also your involvement with the Ella O'Brien case.'

'There's also that.'

'Mr Quinn, there's quite a lot of ground to cover here. Most of it is out of jurisdiction and happened a very long time ago and until we listen to the tapes we ask that you remain in Ireland. In the meantime, we are going to have to ask for the passport you travelled on? Travelling under a false identity is an offence.'

'Of course.'

'And also insist that you do not leave this ward until given permission to do so? Do you understand this and agree to comply?'

'I'm an old man. I'm not going to run anywhere. I came back to sort through all of this. I wish to help in any way I can.'

'Good. Good.'

'I would ask, though, that I could travel to see Ella at the convent?'

They aren't sure what to say.

'I wouldn't expect to cause any more trouble.'

'We can see if that would be possible, Mr Quinn.'

'Call me Charlie. I've missed my real name.'

'We can see if we can grant that request, Mr Quinn.'

53

CHARLIE QUINN

The private hospital room isn't small and I miss the noise and space of the public ward.

'It's for your own privacy,' the nurse manager says. 'And you won't need to go to the Garda station if they can come here to speak with you. It's best for everyone.'

'I'm in a type of prison. I don't like feeling hemmed in,' I reply. She is of no assistance and opens the small window before slamming the door on her way out.

When I turn on Rhonda's recorder, I go away to the prairies of the 1940s.

I had become aware of some of what Ella went through since I left. There were immigrants from Ireland flowing into Canada and her name was easy to slip into conversations. She was a legend for all the wrong reasons and I listened and asked a few questions here and there. Keeping quiet about what I knew wasn't to protect myself, you understand. In Canada, I was well away from the threats of prison and all of that, and I wasn't sure what she would need of me in the future. The general public had made up their minds about the guilt and who was responsible. It seemed once things were quiet and she was safe in the convent, there was no need to drag up the whole thing all over again.

A little part of me considered that the Mrs O'Brien in the newspapers and on everyone's lips wasn't even my Ella. What I mean is, I was a young boy and my Ella was like a dream, a muse, a reason for living. The Ella I made in my head and heart might not have been a true person. For surely a whole nation of people wouldn't condemn the beautiful, innocent woman that I knew?

In those early days in Canada, when the homesickness was fierce, I thought about racing homewards and rescuing her. Then a doubt would surface about whether the baby was even mine. I would call myself a fool, like her husband had called me.

Even if I hadn't fallen into taking another man's name, coming home to face truths was much too scary then. It was easier to keep seeing the beauty of our lives together and to throw out all of the sadness.

Hiding everything, even from myself, was better than blaming my own stupidity. If I let in the truth then I would have had to come to terms with the fact that I did not protect Ella and our baby that day. If I pretended that Ella was indeed guilty, I wasn't the scared boy who left her to her fate.

Now I know that unless I accept the decisions I made throughout my life, I'll never be able to help Ella.

54

CHARLIE QUINN

E lla is refusing to see me. I've rung the number and written to the address. Both times I'm told that she has no further interest in speaking with Charlie Quinn.

This seems unlikely. She was a bit cold-hearted when I met her, and that was understandable. She didn't know then that I had come to rescue her. She's had time to think about it now and will see that I'm working everything around to fix things.

There have been articles in newspapers about how women fall from one abusive relationship into another. It alludes to Ella's need for controlling men and how she was downtrodden into losing her sense of motherhood. I was shaken by the ones on how delinquency is linked to stalking and in some cases serial-killing. The one on cases of medical professionals getting god-complexes and using their status to hide crimes was particularly interesting. There were, of course, those on women in history who were tried for infanticide and even more conjecture on what drove them to it.

The nation is trying to come to a conclusion again. There are lessons to be learned and questions to be answered and they aim to find the solution and round it off in a nice, neat bow.

The Gardai are professionals and I like to see them coming. The four walls are boring and there's a rush on my conscience to get the whole thing finished with. If only Ella would let me know what she needs me to do. If only I knew what the best direction was. I've waited this long and there will be only one chance to do this right – for my Ella and Maeve.

The noise of the record button takes me into the past immediately. Rhonda has asked to join the questioning and she wants to return to certain places that she needs clarification on. Strangely, the police think she will keep me calm and talkative. She's given us a list and this is more off-putting than they all realise. I'm used to a flow of memories and this list is not appreciated. I don't want to talk about the death of my mother. However, it is on this list.

Taking a deep breath, I start – 'My father made me help him dispose of my mother's murdered corpse in the quarry. Beth Quinn was my mother and her death traumatised us all. Cedric suspected that Father had killed her. I never told him or anyone else the truth. There was no way to bring Mammy back and I was a bold child known for being a handful. Telling lies came easy to me, everyone knew that. If I accused Father and was proved right, we'd all have been destined to end up in the homes we were threatened with on a regular basis. If I was disbelieved, Father might have killed me like he threatened – or worse still, he might have hurt Cedric and Anna. I was never asked if I knew anything about my mother's passing. I simply lied with a silence and buried the reality with her.

'From that moment on, Father reformed a bit and I could escape him. The crime drifted away and I only got an odd nightmare and a tug on the soul. I put it behind me because I was a growing boy with a future to create.

'Cuff me now for not coming forward or understanding what was going on in the mind of a ten-year-old child.'

'And this is the truth?' Rhonda asks. 'Might you have killed her yourself?'

Rhonda blurs into a watery shape and the next droplet moves to take its place. 'It never occurred to me that anyone would think that I killed Mammy,' I say, barely able to breathe. 'I'll try to read the list and get this over with. Randal Hamilton and his fucking coat – this thin boy stood out as a weakling. If I hadn't taken his clothes then someone else would have. I didn't know him well enough. At the time, I didn't feel bad about what I did. He was younger than me and put up a good fight. I'll give him that. He said it was his dead father's coat and that should have stopped me. I was cold in every sense. I knew the coat would fit me as it was much too big for this weakling child. I was a bad bastard to take it.'

Rhonda sits taller and says, 'I had difficulty finding him as you stood into the official photograph. He was on the ship's manifesto and was not registered working anywhere in Canada.'

'You thought I killed him as well?'

'I was concerned until I found Randal. I think I found him. He was Edgar Randal Hamilton, named after his father. He died in the war after working for many years on ranches all over Alberta.'

'I went looking for him once, too, and found his grave,' I tell her. 'I made sure to beg his forgiveness. I felt that I had made my peace with him.'

'Bridget Fahy?'

'Is she next on your precious list?'

'She is.'

'I ran and failed to protect another beautiful creature. I still picture her eating that peach, squatted down, relishing every morsel. She was braver than me. Imagine that.' I look around the room. 'I was a fully-grown man, capable of fathering a child and a small, undernourished girl, eating a peach was stronger than I was.'

'Why did you not try to report Fran Daly?' Rhonda asks.

'How could a youngster report a man with property? Charlie Quinn was on the run from Ireland as it was. After I ran from Daly's in fear I became known as Randal Hamilton who was finally making a life for himself. What would I say that would make anyone believe me? Home-children were a class beneath. Daly was not suspected of any wrongdoing despite many crimes on his land before that. I'm sure Bridget wasn't the first to die. If there are records I'm sure they will prove that children went missing from Daly's before. That rotten pair raised a family and took in waifs and strays. Who or what was I? I'm guilty of the crime of silence again and of running away. It was what I did best in those days. I was a good runner – but I didn't pull that trigger.'

'You left the others behind to suffer?' Rhonda says.

'Thousands of children went through that system. Should I have rescued them all? I was a foolish, cowardly bastard and I was trying to survive.'

'Polly Hollyridge and Gus Kelly,' Rhonda reads off her own list. 'Polly did marry the hotel owner and lived in comfort. She had a stroke at a young age and moved into a care home until she passed away fifteen years ago. According to the staff she had a good quality of life.'

'She had a nice time without me. I'm glad of that.'

'Gus Kelly?' another voice asks.

'Oh now, that bastard is a different story altogether.'

55

CHARLIE QUINN

The barn smelt of shorn hay and there was no nicer smell than a dry, good crop like that. I used to take naps in that hay and sometimes would wrestle Olga into it. Before Gus's death, Olga was driving a new truck of her own. She was the brains behind the meat-packing side of the business. Gus didn't like that and he made things difficult. As usual! He made everything difficult. He roared impossible demands, threw his weight around and generally made our lives miserable.

I could see his resentment growing. He tried to dictate Olga's comings and goings and kept tabs on every move she made. It reminded me of other bad men I knew. The businesses all requested Olga's input. If he did keep her away they asked for her. This drove him stir crazy. Men teased him about the level of work he did in comparison to Olga and I'm sure they taunted him about the money she brought in. It was all getting very tense.

Much as I was intimidated by Ella's husband, Dr O'Brien, I was determined to get the better of Gus Kelly. I saw what being fearful did to my mother and to Ella. I was determined that I would have the upper hand with Gus. There would be no giving up when the time came to tackle that bastard. I wanted to kill him. I planned and practised the act in my head. Of course, I knew it was murder. It was a means to an end. Gus Kelly needed to go and Charlie Quinn was the man to kill him.

It wasn't hard to get Gus into the loft and even easier to push him onto the plough. That was the most satisfying thud. The nicest sound was the strange hiss he made as his breath left. Yes, I murdered Gus Kelly. I did it to take his wife, property and his position as Tom's stepson. I never told a soul that before. There it is – I murdered Gus Kelly and do you know I'm rather proud of the whole thing. Isn't that awful?

Olga possibly guessed – we never discussed it. I'd like to think that she loved me more for doing it. Tom might have suspected it too. He and Gus never got along. The men were scared sufficiently of me afterwards to do all the work given to them and I grew ten feet with the thoughts of getting away with it.

Why admit to it now, you may well ask? I want it to be known that Charlie Quinn is not a liar. All truths must come out – or none at all. I'm saying it for Olga's sake too. Yes, she is still living. With all that is coming forward for my Ella, I want Olga to know that I killed for her. Olga is waiting on Kelly's homestead in Canada. We are more friends than anything. Companions. She is more than used to me being away for months at a time and this trip was only something she raised an eyebrow to. There weren't many questions. Olga has always thought that I wanted the land more than her, and that's not strictly true. When Gus thumped off that metal, it was also to free us both to be together.

I wasn't the best husband. Olga deserves to know that the man she married can take ownership of his past with her too. I'm dying and I don't care if I rot in hell for that deed. I've not regretted it – not for one minute. I have many regrets. Gus

Kelly's death is not one of them. I'll never need to atone for that crime. Never!

The unease is something I can taste. Taking a glance at the list, I know it is time to discuss the mystery around Ella.

'I wish I could speak with Ella, before I answer any more questions and hand over the conversation we shared together.'

Rhonda is the one to answer me first although many open their mouths at the same time. 'She sent a short message. I can give you the open note in her handwriting. She has asked for you to tell the truth.'

Closing out the people in the room, I open the folded paper and there is the swirled letters spelling out what she needs.

Dearest Charlie,

I've missed you more than words can say and I don't know where to begin.

I want to thank you for coming to Ireland to tell the truth after all these years.

I never discussed my first two darling babies with you. They were stillborn. I couldn't dwell on such things. When I fell pregnant with Maeve I was happy with you and I was always honest.

Our Maeve was born healthy and I feel in my heart that my husband, Dr Jeremiah O'Brien murdered her. He smothered her. I could not do such a thing. For many years now, his family have felt this too, and they have tried to help me.

Charlie, you are not to blame, there was nothing we could have done. All I need from you, my love, is that you tell the truth. Tell your truth and let the rest fall into place. There should be no more lies.

You are the love of my life – now and forever more,

Ella x

I go back to where we were our best. We are in my bed. She's laughing at one of my stories and I have a hand over her mouth to quieten her down. We are young and happy.

Neither of us wanted the baby at the start. She thought that if she cared then the outcome would be bad. She didn't want to be upset all over again. I wasn't sure what it would all mean. Over time, I came to like the idea and the growing swell. I thought I would own someone. The baby would be mine and then after a bit of work Ella would be all mine too. Plans hatched as to how I would make this work.

For too long, I'd let other men, like my father and Jock, take charge of my happiness. I'd won Ella over and that had taken time and patience. If I worked hard then the best would come.

It didn't seem wrong to follow Ella and watch over her. It didn't seem wrong to imagine killing that bad husband and taking her away with me either. My plans to seduce Ella worked and the only thing was I had no notion of what was to come because of it.

The day Ella went into labour I panicked. Things were not ready for our escape. I had failed to fully admit to Ella that I was actively planning our flit from Ireland. Some things were organised for a few weeks' time but the baby was coming. How I thought Ella would pop out a baby and then simply jump on a ship with me – I'll never know. They were the immature thoughts I had.

Ella left my lodgings distressed for many reasons. I was being a child and she was having one. As soon as she had gone, I slunk after her, like I usually did. I was ashamed that I followed her home, and listened to all that was going on, and that I let bad things happen right under my nose. Whatever he was going to do, I left him to it. In all my tall tales I could never have dreamt up what he did next.

Confronting the good doctor was not in the plan. I didn't do a very good job of it. I was a frightened child and he was a confident killer. He said awful things and I ran from the house, before I saw or held my own child.

I don't think I need to spell it out what he must have done when I put my tail between my legs and scuttled away. The authorities say that the child was suffocated after birth. Ella had no reason to do such a thing. Even if she was capable of it, which she wasn't, Ella was not able to do that. Jeremiah always threatened to destroy Ella. He was a person people believed, a man of prestige with a wealthy family. He had people around him who knew the law and how to bend it.

I know he died last year. I checked before I came back. He had no other children and I'm sure Ella saw her opportunity now to clear her own name. She hasn't directly accused him and I wish that she did. It might seem strange to others that she doesn't scream her accusations. But I see her plight with this. Ella knows what it is like to be accused of terrible things, and despite everything, without evidence, she cannot bring herself to do the same to him. I really want to have the proof she needs. I could say that I saw him harm our child. This would help us – but that would be more lies. I could say that I harmed our baby – and that would be untrue. Ella has asked me to do one last thing and that is to tell the truth – and I will honour her wishes.

Up until now, I have left large bits of my life open to interpretation. I needed to wait. I didn't know what Ella might need me to do. I thought she would want me to finally come forward and lie. I was wrong. I suspected that she'd ask me to be untruthful about that day. Charlie Quinn has always been a good liar and if I could help Ella I would lie many times over.

I can't do that now – not after that note.

I thought that she might let me shoulder the blame. I thought that she'd finally be protected, finally let me set her free from all of this. I'm a man who hid murders, a man capable of horrible things – one more despicable act, for my Ella, would have been okay in my books.

That's not to be either.

I've come all of this way, and waited sixty years to tell the truth. And here it all is. I hoped to find proof about what her husband did. He never slipped up, and like my own father, he worked hard on making himself a more plausible man. A woman would not be believed. As the years passed it seemed less and less likely that the evidence would emerge. I thought if a rich Canadian rancher, with nothing to gain and everything to lose came back and said what Ella needed him to say then it all would work out. I thought that a good woman might be saved if a dying old cowboy came home and told his version of things. I've wanted nothing else for a long time – I finally thought I'd get to ride in on my horse and save the woman I love.

I want to go back in time and see that day all over again. I want to know how to disprove that man who took everything from us. I don't know how to destroy him without lying. Finally, I have done what Ella wants.

'You know nothing more?' Rhonda asks.

'I hope that I've shown you the truth. That should be enough.'

56

RHONDA IRWIN

Charlie is heading home to Canada and he must be exhausted for I am wrecked. Joe has been such a support. Charlie is all alone.

'He's used to it. Expected it,' Joe says as we sit into a taxi. He takes my hand in his and Faye runs her fingers into my hair as she sits high on my lap.

'Ella finally accused her husband. Isn't it odd that she went through all of that and he wasn't considered a suspect?'

'Yes, it was the way things were,' Joe says after telling the driver we want to go to the airport. 'How sad that Charlie has to go back to Canada. He'll have no time to spend with Ella now. Do you think they'll ever see each other again?'

'I doubt it. You know I cannot write about all of this. I'm not objective anymore,' I admit. 'I'm too close to it and it makes me emotional. I'd not do it justice.'

'Let's wait and see,' Joe says. 'I'm going to have no work leave left and with Faye going to the new childminder soon – you might get some headspace for it?'

'Maybe.'

'Unless we decide to get married and have another baby?' Joe smiles. 'Marry me, Rhonda?'

The driver coughs and Faye squeals to be let over onto Daddy's knee. It's the last thing I thought he'd say today of all days.

'Do you mean it?'

'Of course I do.'

'Married?'

'I should have asked you a long time ago.'

'I love you, Joe.'

'That will help. I love you too. Is it a yes then?'

'Yes.'

Faye says, 'Yes, yes, yes.'

Silently, I look into the traffic and thank Charlie Quinn.

57

CHARLIE QUINN

Ella has agreed to see me before my departure. Rhonda and Joe are embarrassed by the people staring at us. My photograph and some facts have been released to the media. I have promised to go to the Canadian authorities once I get off the plane I'm about to board.

Faye plays with the buttons on the jacket Rhonda gave me. Talking into Faye's fine hair I say, 'Thank you, precious, for beginning all of this. Without you I might not have found the strength to start.' Turning to Rhonda I add, 'I would not have managed to do all of this without you either. Thank you for putting up with me. I'll be in touch when I get back.' I look away when they shake my hand. There are no words left in me. I am watching my Ella get wheeled closer.

She's pushed by the same nice lady.

There's a flickering of hope that Ella will be vindicated and the relief is immense. The intern was found out as the snitch who sold the photograph of our meeting. We've been told that he has been let go. The company said too that they would like to start work with Rhonda soon on my story. The nice lady nods to Rhonda as they pass.

'I've been listening to your account of things. I'm proud of you, Charlie,' Ella says when we are parked together. The nice lady pretends not to listen as Ella leans closer. 'I was glad you agreed that I could listen to the tapes. I love hearing your voice.'

'They said I could get a copy of yours too – when you do them. I'll need the distraction if they lock me up. Did they tell you about me murdering a man? I'm hoping I have a long trial as the size of the cells frightens me.'

'We don't have much time. Let's talk about nice things,' she says.

Ella's dress is a lovely shade of red under the navy cardigan. Her hair is tied back from her face, just how I like it. She's had her nails painted to match her dress. I kiss those fingertips. Our fingers wind around each other and we sit like this for a good long time. Precious moments go too quickly. I cannot lose her all over again, but it is happening.

'At least we have a chance to say goodbye this time,' I add.

Ella rubs the back of my hand. 'Thank you, Charlie. Thank you for loving me enough to come back. Thank you for trying to help.'

'It just took me sixty years.'

'That doesn't matter. You did what you could, that's all that matters. And look what happened to you because of it? Canadian and Irish police? Is all of that necessary?'

'I warned them that I wouldn't make it easy. I told them that a wily old cowboy might be hard to lasso if he escaped. Anyhow, I know Olga will enjoy thinking that I'm a wanted man. She's always liked the movies and drama.'

Ella giggles.

'It's true though. I'm not sure how I'll leave you again. They may have to drag me away.'

'This is hard.'

'I should have stayed quiet. We might have been able to be

together if I lied some more. I thought you'd at least let me save you with the bits of my stories. I would do anything for you. I should have said I saw Jeremiah do it.'

'There have been enough lies.'

'If you weren't bothered by a few more, we might have had a chance to be together for longer. I did what you asked and now I'm summoned back to Canada.'

'Thank you for everything.'

'Will you visit?' I ask, already knowing the answer. 'I'd like you to meet Olga and to see the prairies.'

She shakes her darling head and dabs at those beautiful eyes.

'You could lie and tell me that you'll try to come.'

'I can't.' Her tears are flowing now, making her embarrassed.

'I have always thought of Maeve,' I admit, starting to cry too. 'And my love for you has never ended and it never will.'

'It was lost to us both for a long time.'

We agree by holding tightly to each other. I can smell her hair, sense the sadness and I cannot cope with it. 'I'm glad that people know more about what happened. It was worth it,' I say to try to make sense of things.

'It is time to say goodbyes now. You'll need to go through to departures,' the nice lady says. 'We'll look after her, Charlie. Did Ella tell you who I am?'

I search Ella's face for clues.

The nice lady extends a hand and leans on my arm. 'I am one of the O'Brien family's legal team. For quite some time there's been upset in O'Brien circles about the way Ella was treated. The present generation wants to put things right. We will do all that we can to help clear Ella's name.'

'The O'Brien's knew the truth all along? They knew?'

'The family did more for Ella than many people realise,' she replies. 'They always hoped that Dr O'Brien might come forward, as you have done. There was a hope that he would have told the truth. Unfortunately, he did not oblige. I want to let you know that we believe you both.'

'It gives me great relief to know that Ella has people who will protect her. Look after my darling.'

Ella lets go of my hand. I cannot bear it. I lean shakily forward to kiss the lips I adore.

One.

Last.

Time.

We are back on my bed – just like we were.

'I love you,' I tell her.

Ella smiles. 'You are the love of my life, Charlie Quinn – now and forever more.'

THE END

AUTHOR'S NOTE

The Quiet Truth is based on actual historical events. During the research, I found information on the British Home Children in Canada, and women convicted of infanticide in Ireland. Every author likes to feel that their research is good, and I tried to be accurate. Any errors are unintentional or used for fictional effect.

Charlie Quinn was inspired by a man who came into my life as a child. He, like Charlie, came home to Ireland after sixty mysterious years in the Canadian Rockies. With very little known about his life, this gentle man took me for a walk up the road. My storyteller father inspires a great deal of my work and when he sparked off this memory, the totally fictional Charlie Quinn was born.

While looking into Canadian history, I found that over a hundred thousand children were sent right across Canada to be used as indentured servants from the mid 1800s - 1900s. Canadians thought that they were orphaned children, but only a small percentage were. However well-intentioned this process was supposed to be, the majority of children's lives were full of ill-health, neglect, abuse and sometimes death. A life in Canada was supposed to be an appealing option for parents who were struggling with poverty or difficult circumstances. Yet, these children were sent alone, or were separated from their siblings. Some were adopted and accepted into loving families, but many were deeply traumatised and never spoke about their childhoods. The British Home Children, and those like them, have their own quiet truth.

This novel also covers the past of Ella O'Brien, a fictional convicted child murderer in 1930s Ireland. I was shocked that infanticide, or the murder of children by their mother, was more prolific than I imagined. I suppose mercy was shown when most of the women sentenced to death in Ireland were given a reprieve. Some were released into the care of religious orders and many were tried without the presence of a body, and on the say so of family members and neighbours. Incredibly, in most cases, the fathers are also missing from the records and trials. I deliberately wanted this novel told from a man's perspective for this very reason.

Thank you for reading *The Quiet Truth* and I would be most grateful if you could leave a review.

ACKNOWLEDGEMENTS

There's a special magic which brings me to write every day. I thank and love this magic with all of my heart.

I acknowledge all those who've taken me this far along the writing road. Those who've pointed me in the right direction and brought me to this destination. Even if you're not specifically mentioned, I am grateful for every purchase, read, review, piece of advice, and kind word.

To you – the reader of this work, I hope you escaped for a while and will want to read more of my short stories or novels. With your help there will be more.

Thank you to the following people for everything they did/do for me: Benji Bennet, Carmel Harrington, all the IWIers, my own online writing group members indulgeinwriting.com, Vanessa Fox O' Loughlin, Heather Norris, Mona Deery, Aishling McMahon, Danny McCarthy (RIP), Ivan Mulcahy, Dr Liam Farrell, all on #WritersWise, and The Extra Special Kids Facebook page, Rian Magee, Linda Green, Amanda J Evans, Jean O'Sullivan, BR Maycock, Suzanne Hull, Marie O'Halloran, Erin Coriell, Kirsten de Bouter Shilliam, Claire Horan, David Lyons,

Sheila Forsey, Emma Hayes, Pamela Hobbs, Pam Lecky, Orla Kelly and Sharon Dempsey. (This list could be endless.)

Thank you to my agent Tracy Brennan and to the great team at Bloodhound Books UK.

To all my friends, family and community who've supported me all the way and the last mention goes to my husband, Brian – thank you for being the love of my life and my best friend.

Printed in Great Britain
by Amazon